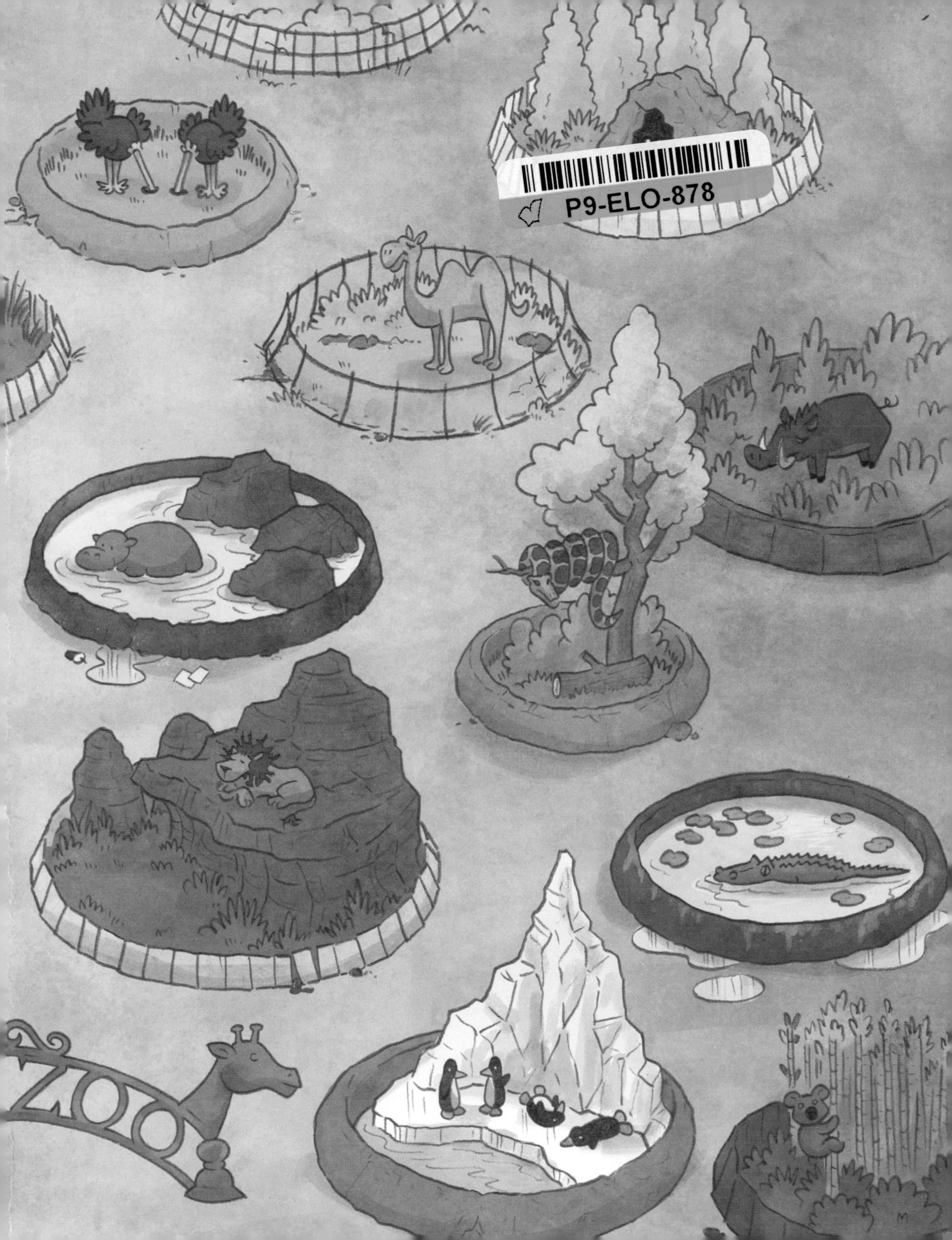
ZOO

HIPPOPOTAMISTER

HIPPOPOTAMISTER

john patrick green

with color by cat caro

First Second
New York

To my favorite thing

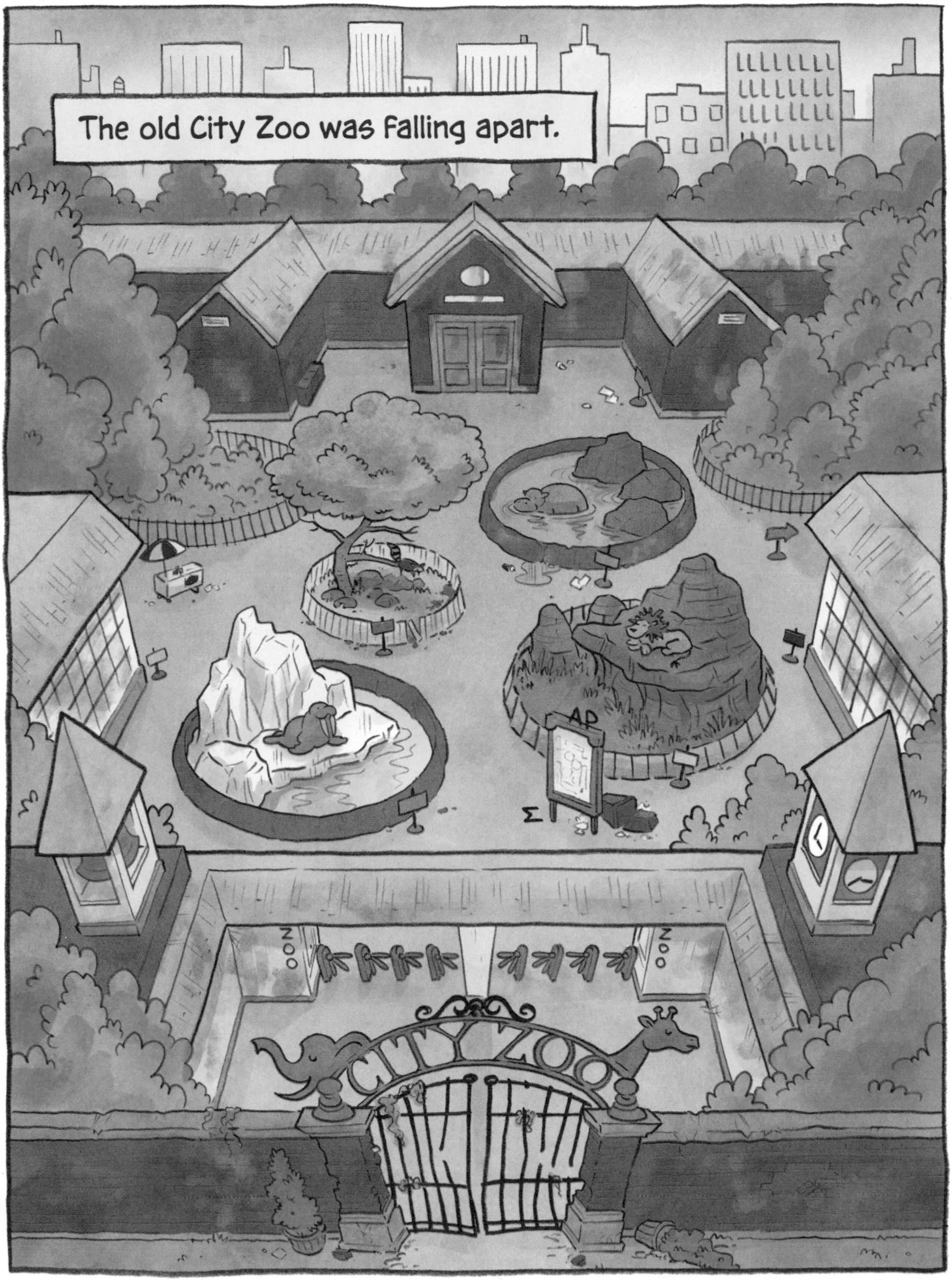
The old City Zoo was falling apart.
CITY ZOO

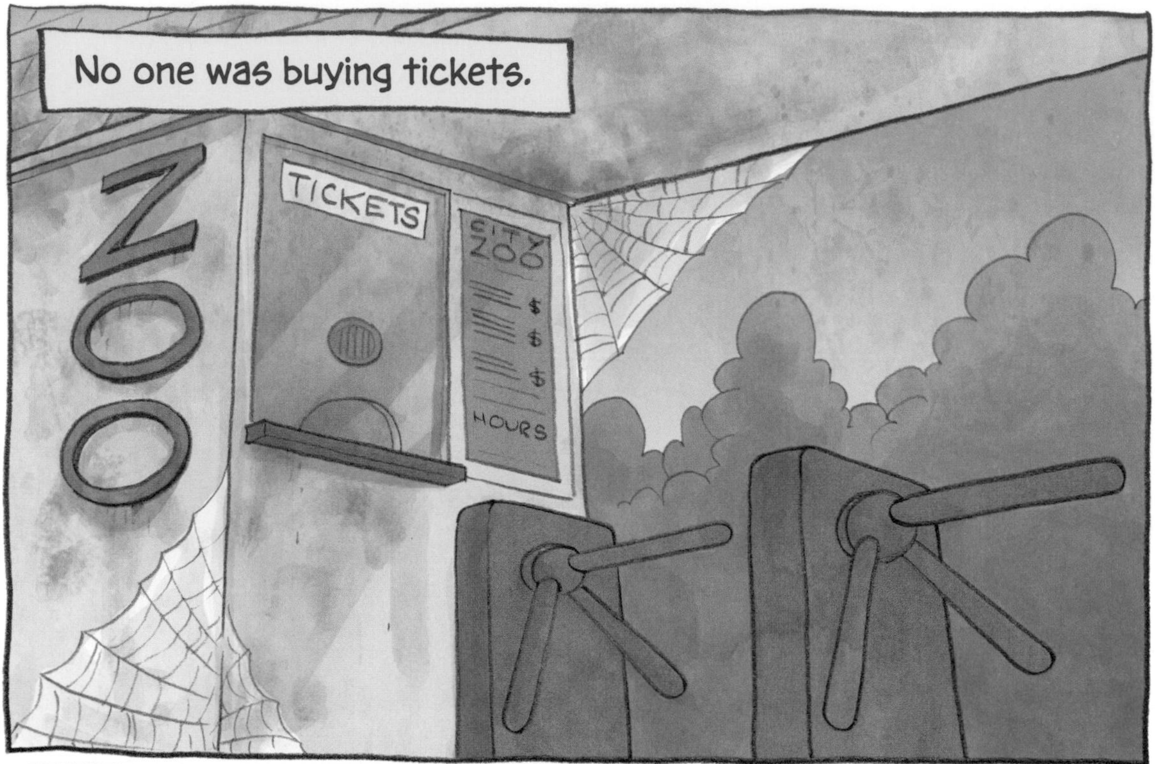
No one was buying tickets.
ZOO
TICKETS
CITY ZOO
$
$
$
HOURS

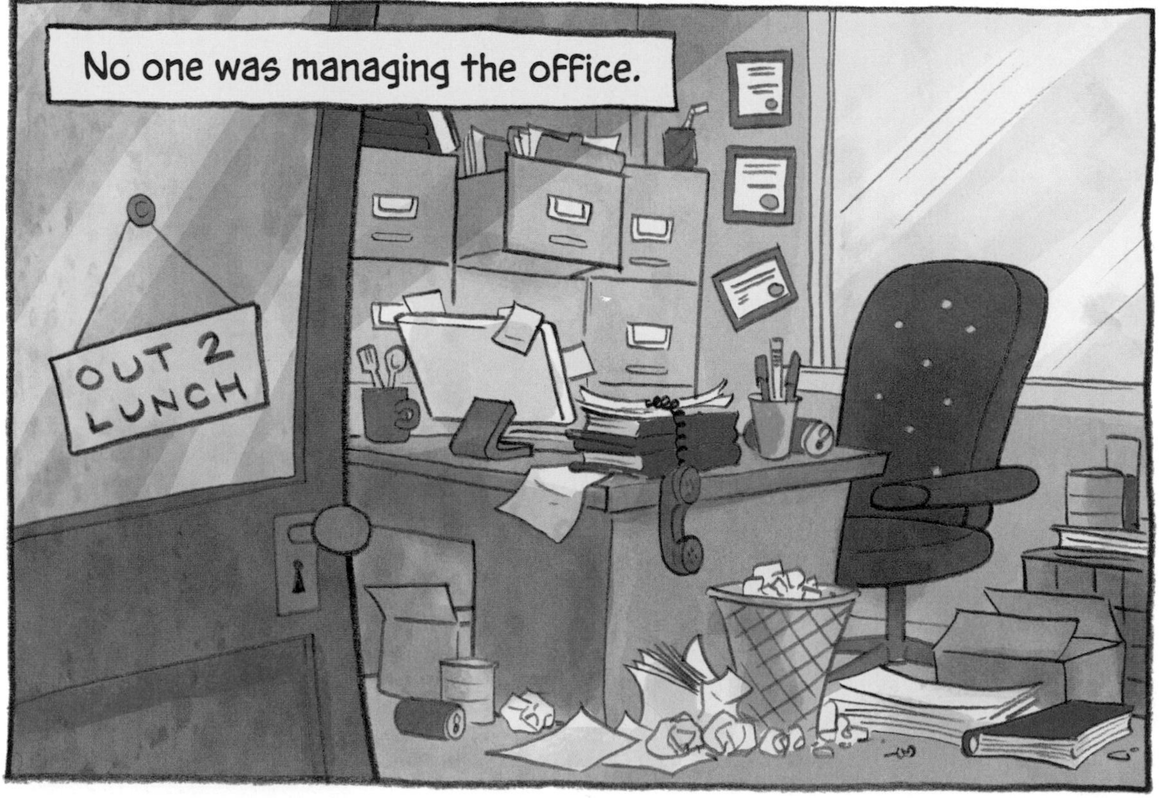
No one was managing the office.
OUT 2 LUNCH

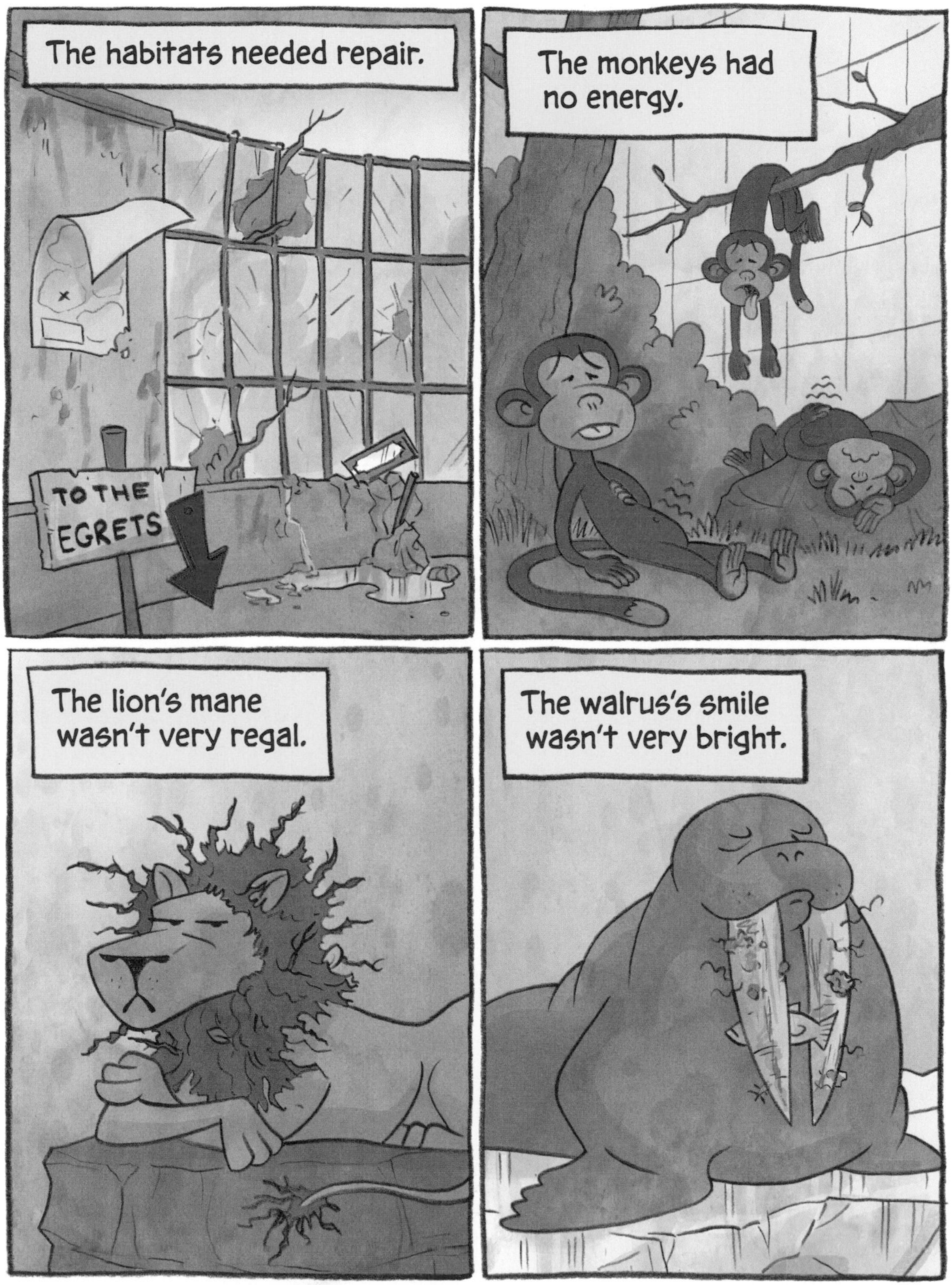
The habitats needed repair.
TO THE EGRETS
The monkeys had no energy.
The lion's mane wasn't very regal.
The walrus's smile wasn't very bright.

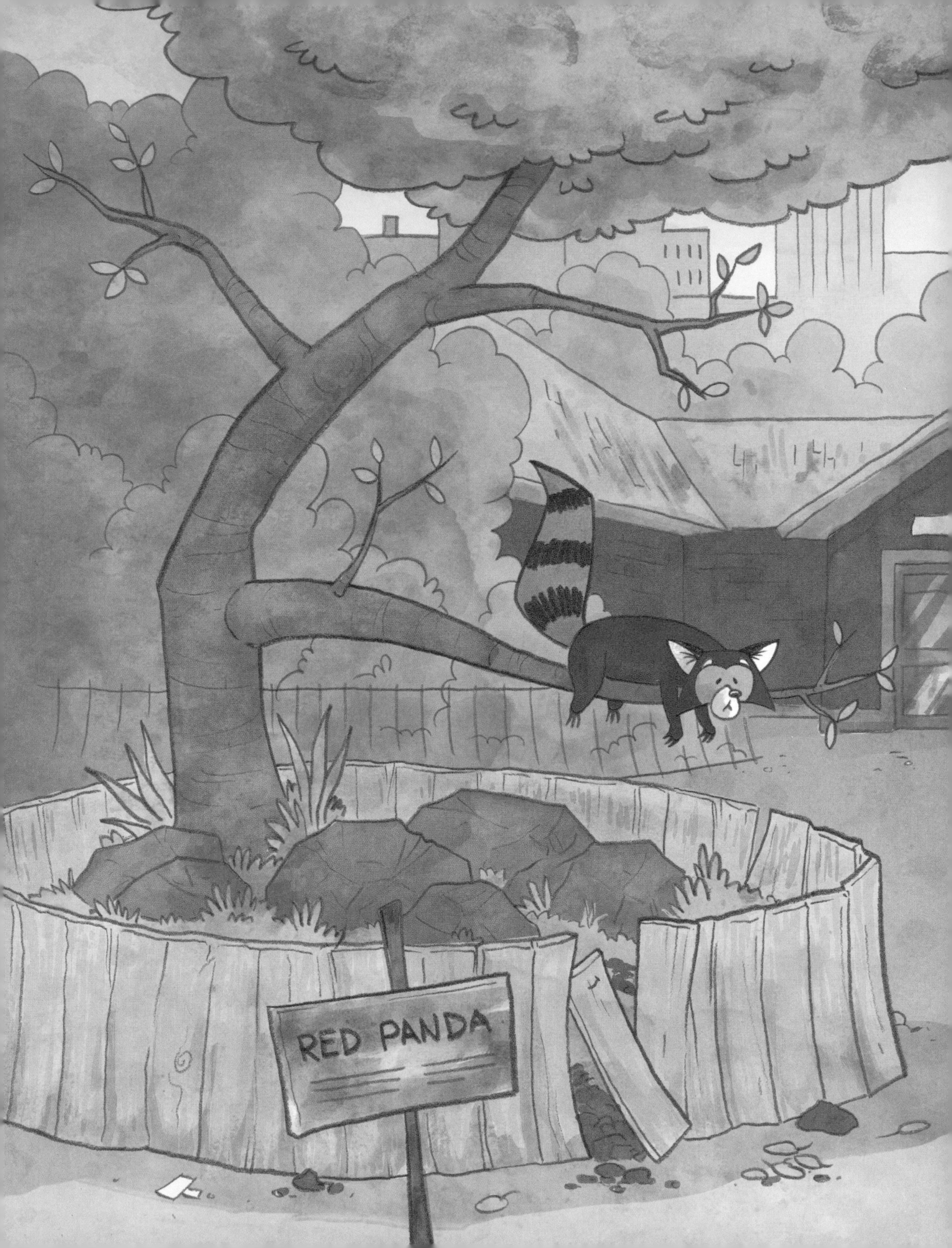
RED PANDA

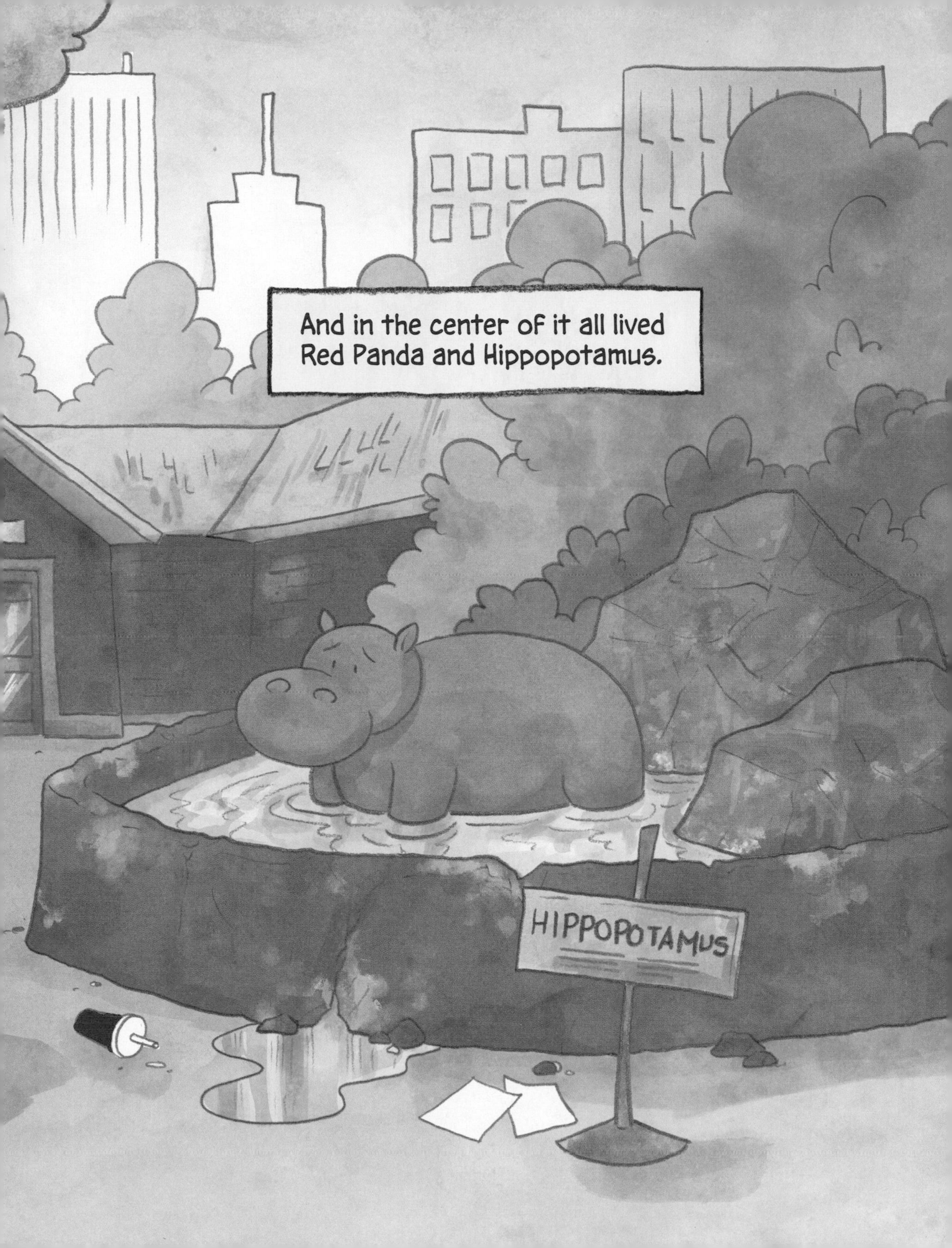
And in the center of it all lived
Red Panda and Hippopotamus.
HIPPOPOTAMUS

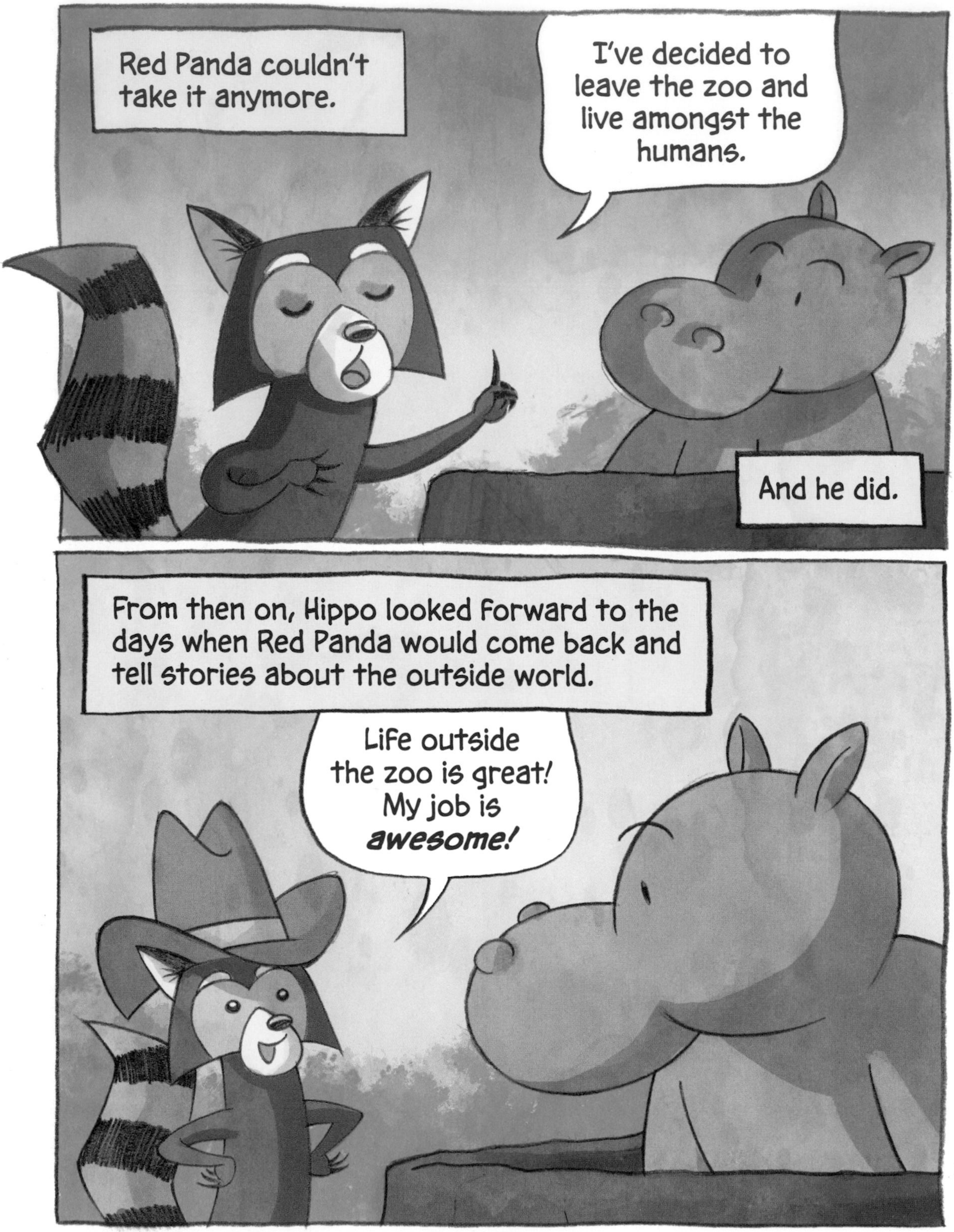
Red Panda couldn't take it anymore.
I've decided to leave the zoo and live amongst the humans.
And he did.
From then on, Hippo looked forward to the days when Red Panda would come back and tell stories about the outside world.
Life outside the zoo is great! My job is ***awesome!***

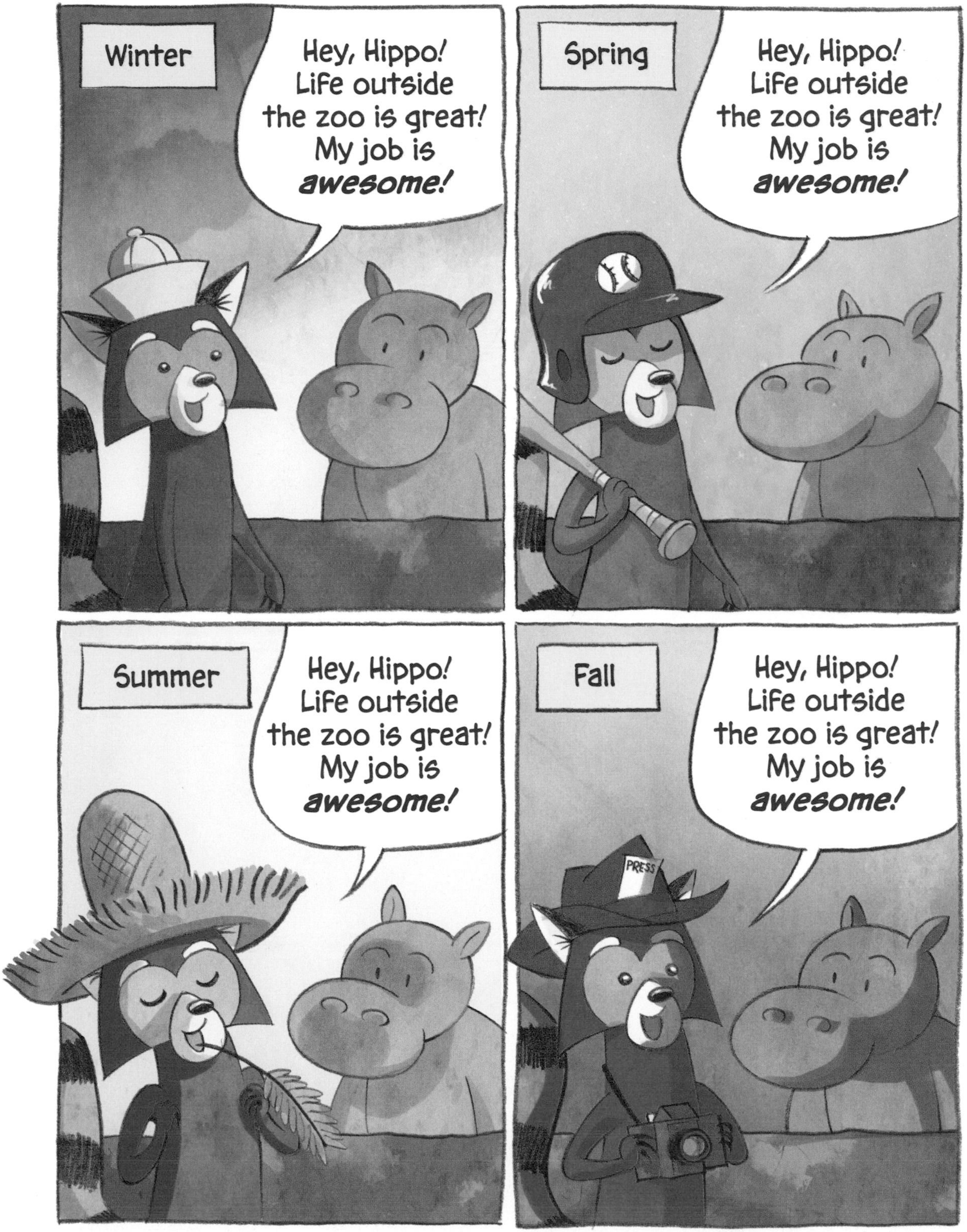
Winter
Hey, Hippo! Life outside the zoo is great! My job is *awesome!*
Spring
Hey, Hippo! Life outside the zoo is great! My job is *awesome!*
Summer
Hey, Hippo! Life outside the zoo is great! My job is *awesome!*
Fall
Hey, Hippo! Life outside the zoo is great! My job is *awesome!*
PRESS

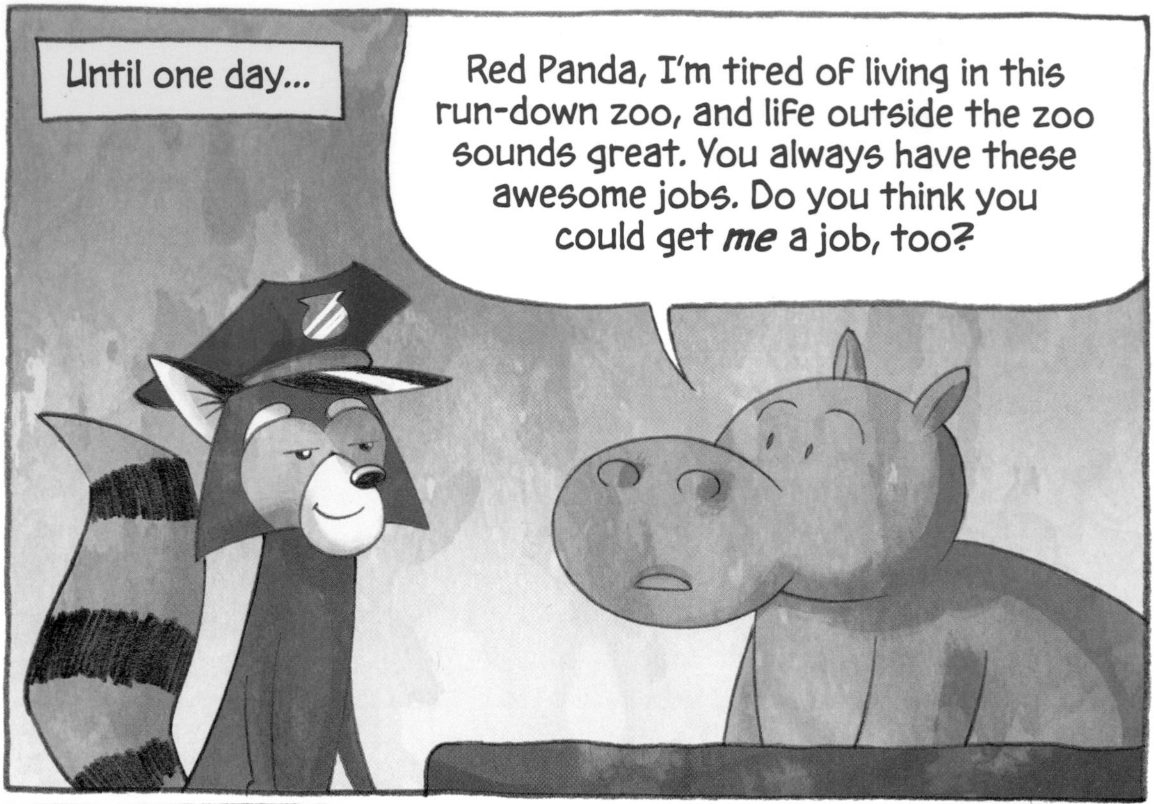
Until one day...
Red Panda, I'm tired of living in this run-down zoo, and life outside the zoo sounds great. You always have these awesome jobs. Do you think you could get *me* a job, too?

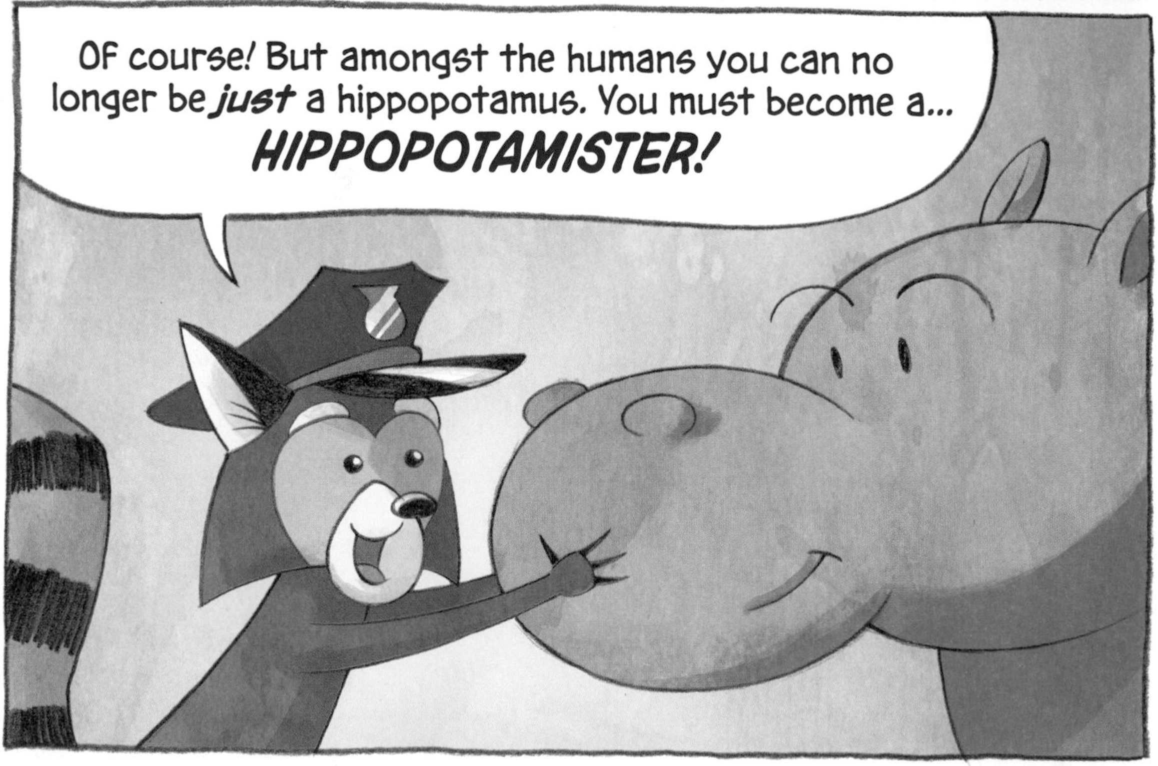
Of course! But amongst the humans you can no longer be *just* a hippopotamus. You must become a...
HIPPOPOTAMISTER!

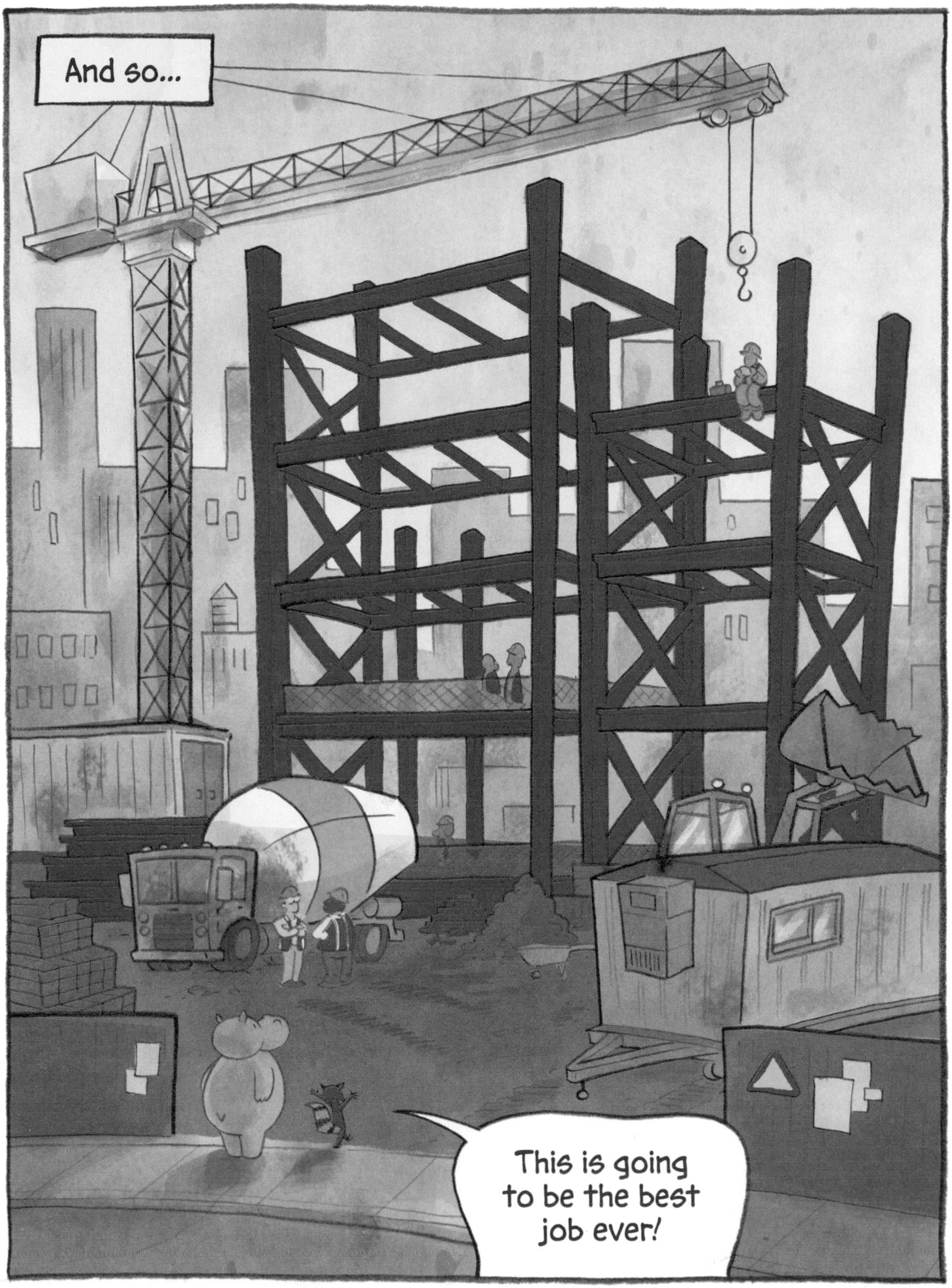
And so...
This is going to be the best job ever!

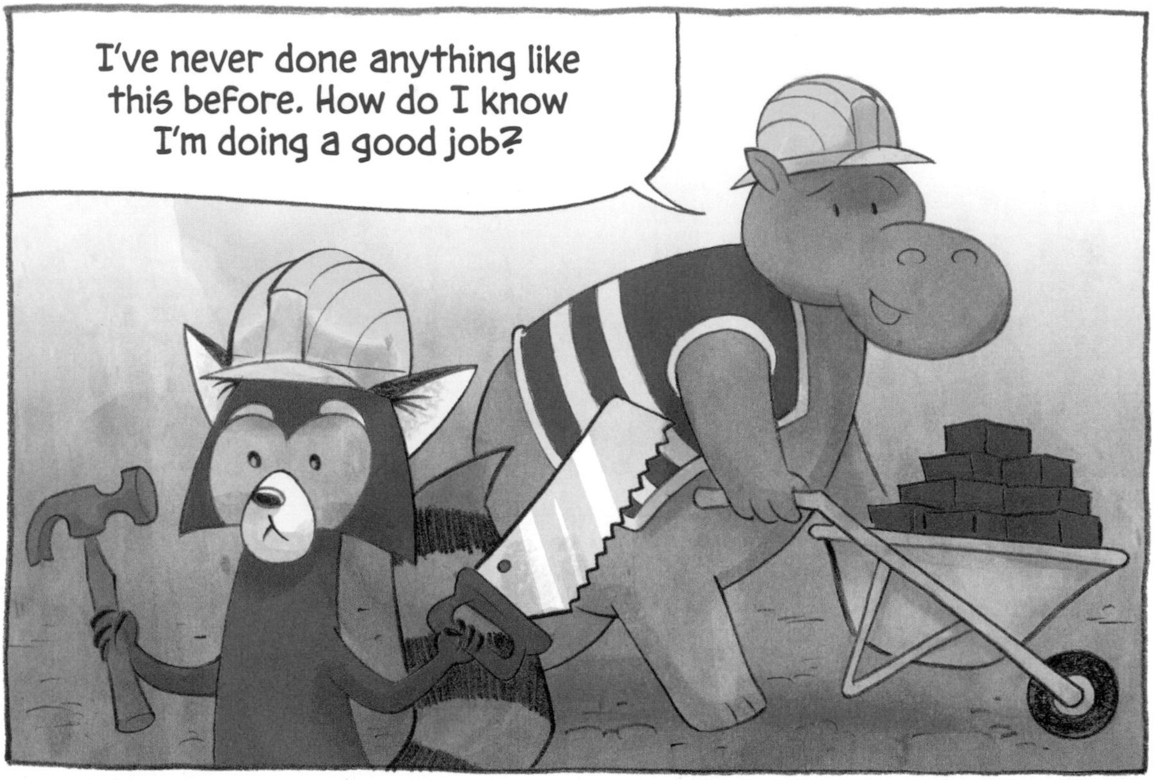
I've never done anything like this before. How do I know I'm doing a good job?

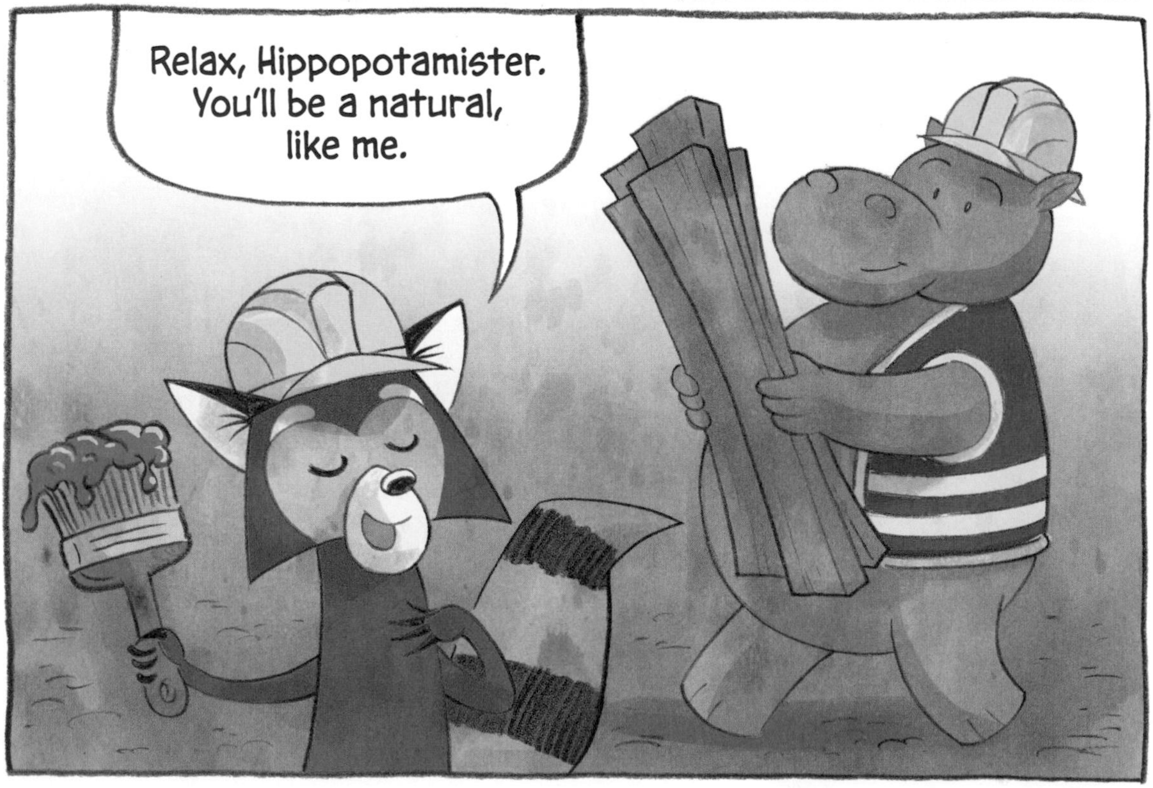
Relax, Hippopotamister. You'll be a natural, like me.

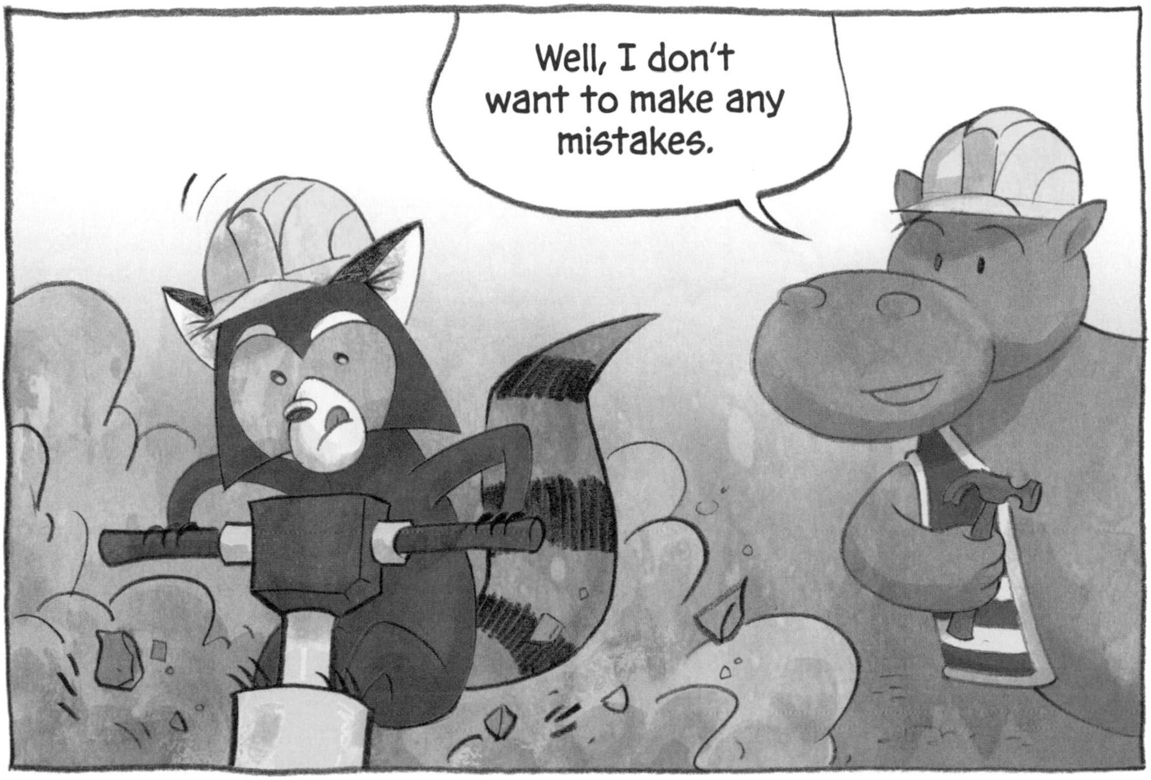
Well, I don't want to make any mistakes.

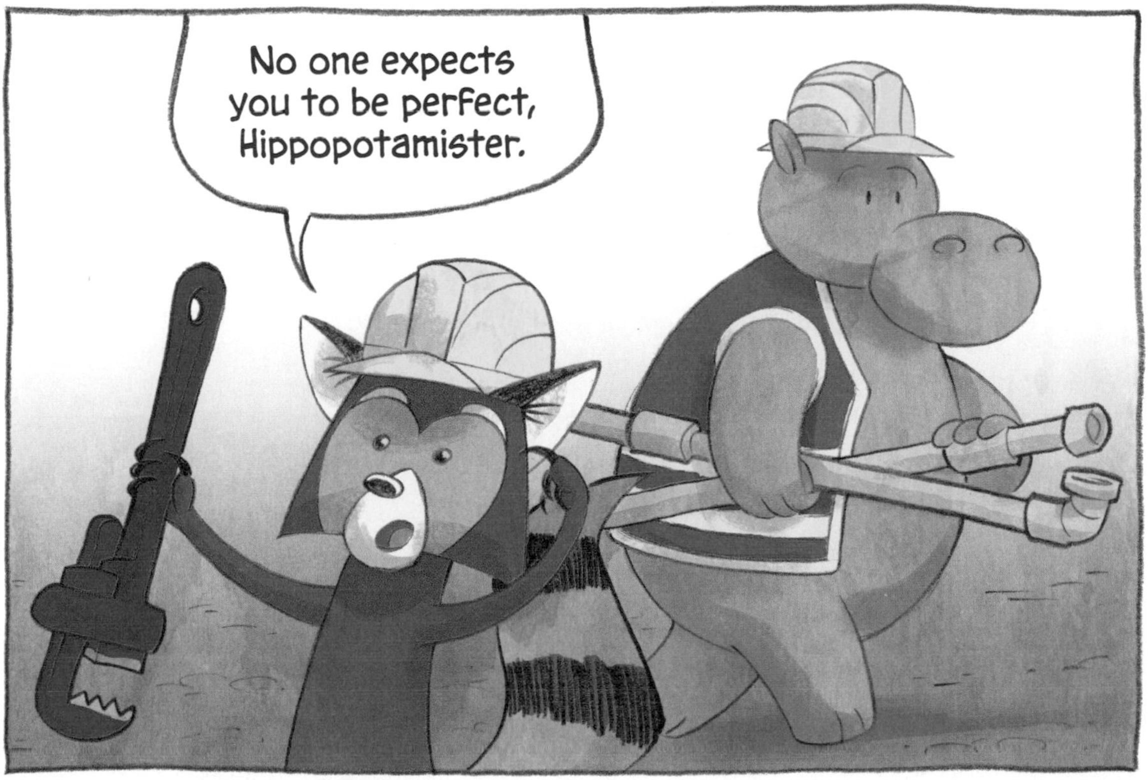
No one expects you to be perfect, Hippopotamister.

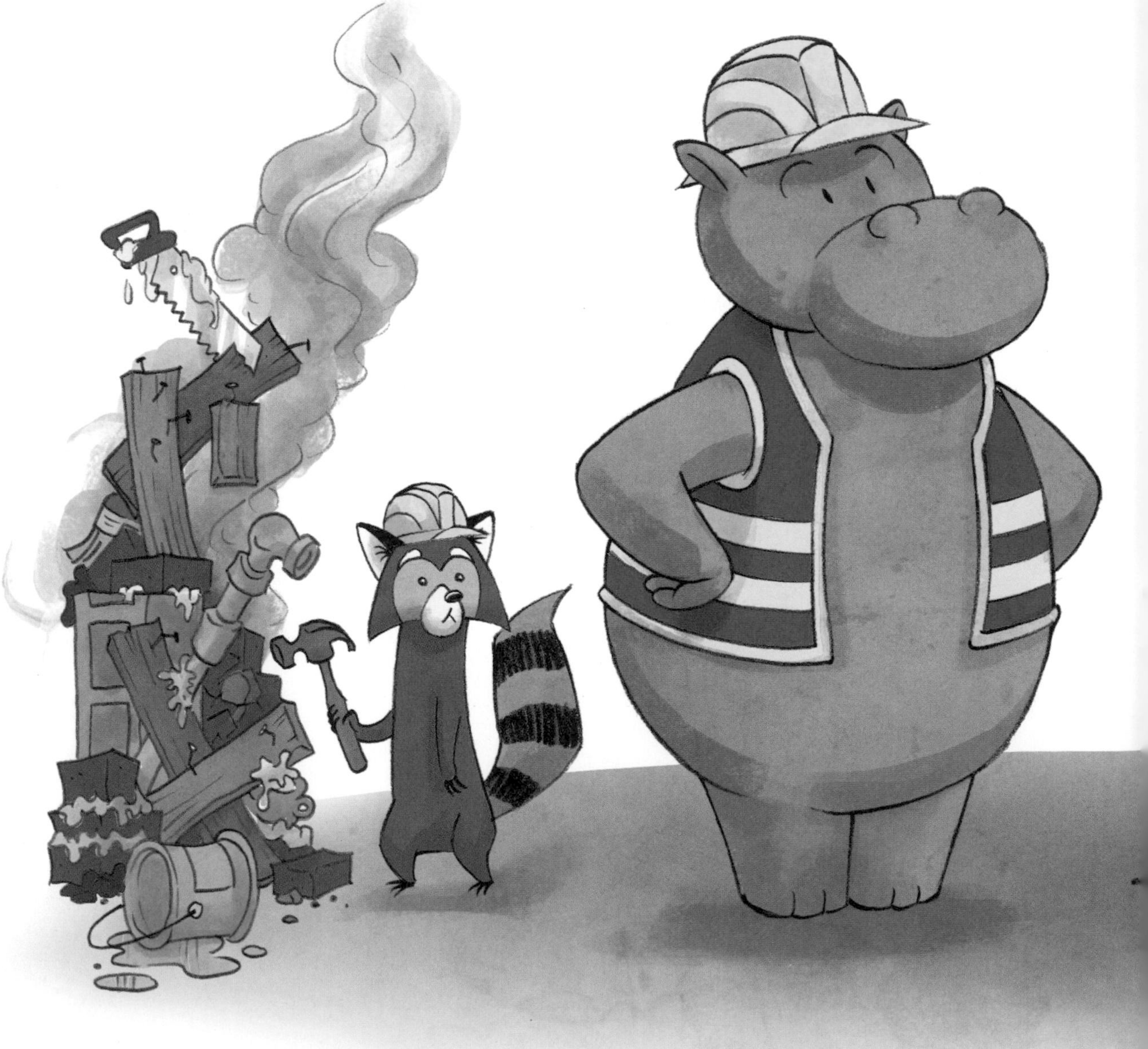

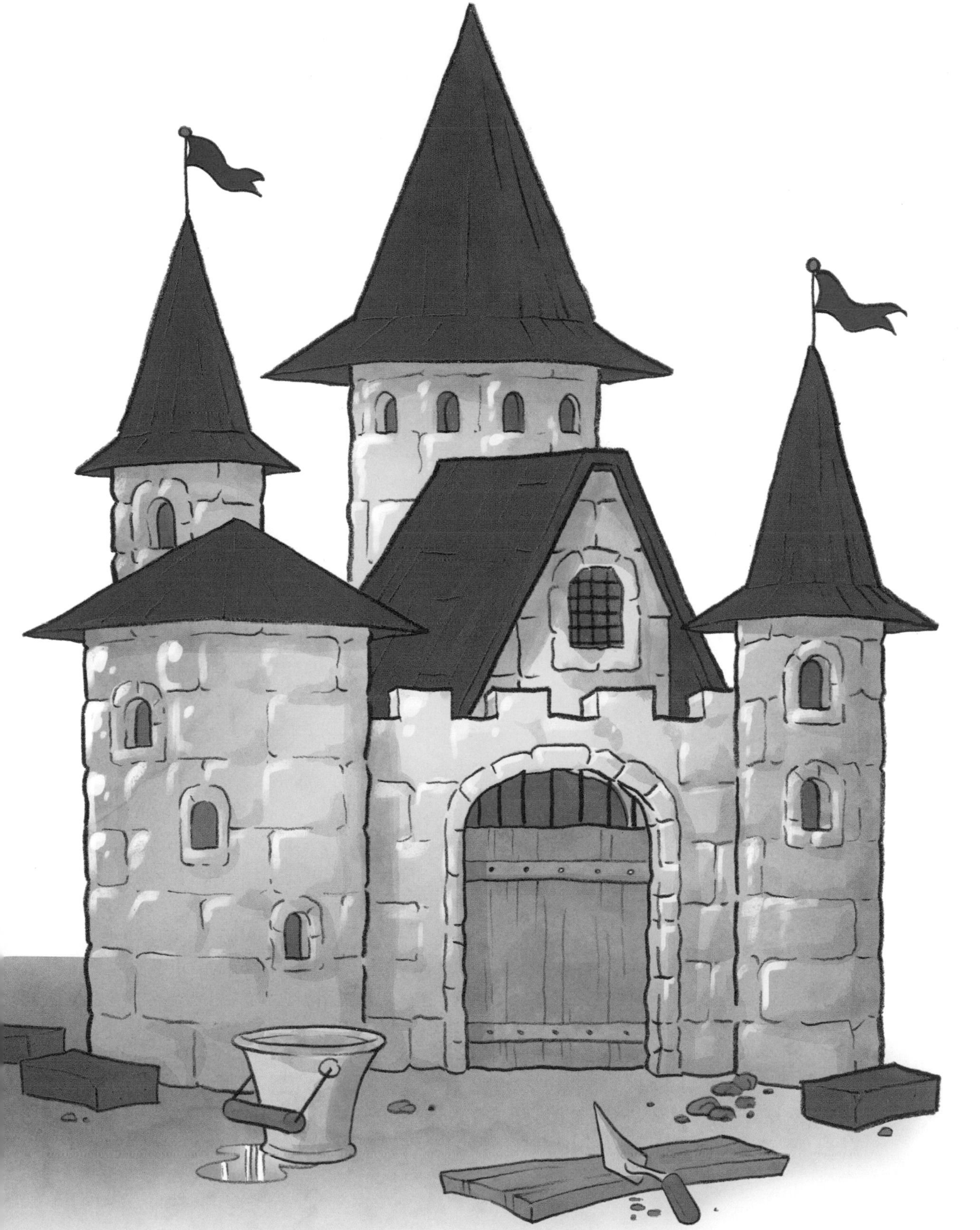

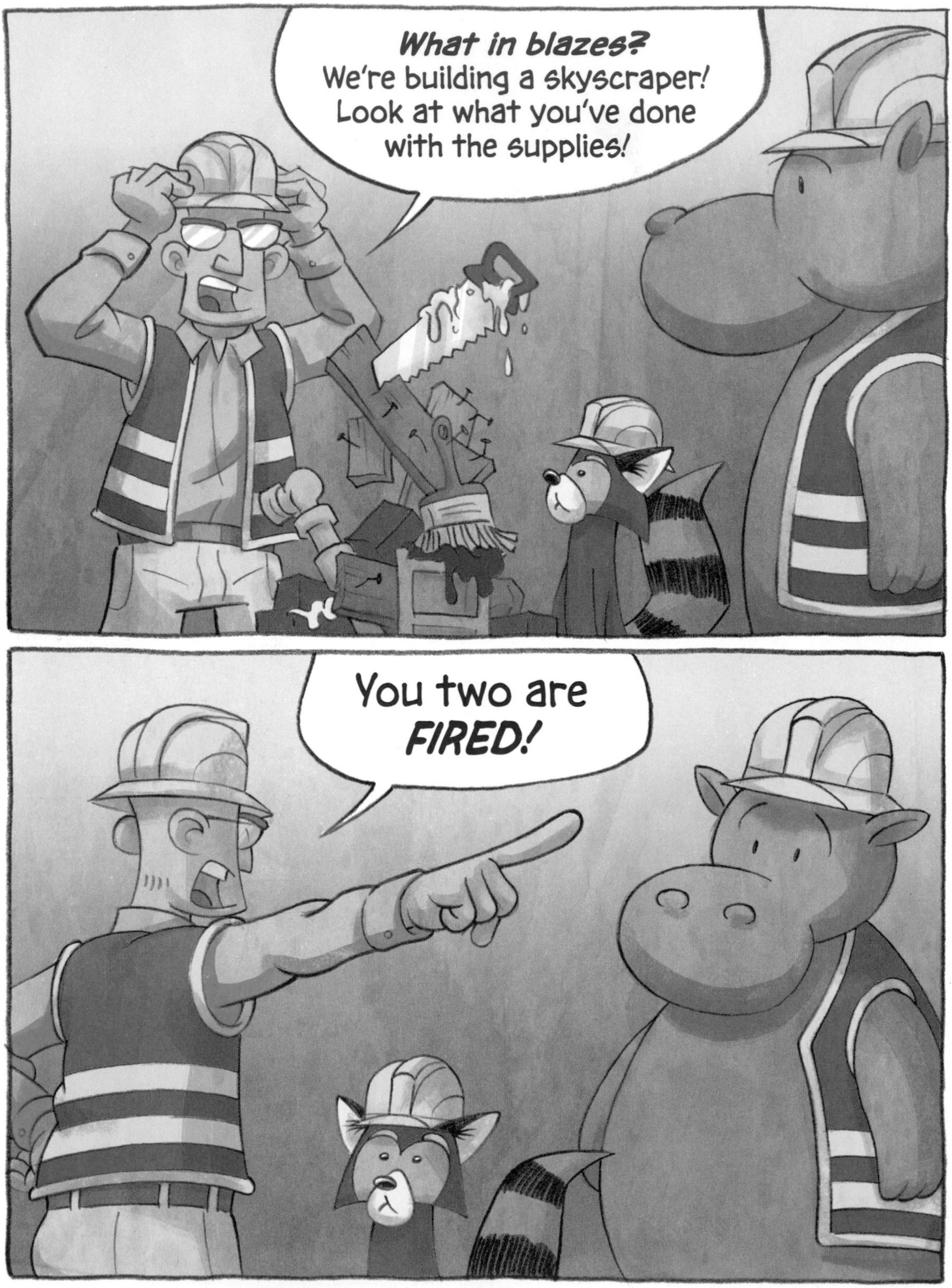

What in blazes? We're building a skyscraper! Look at what you've done with the supplies!
You two are *FIRED!*

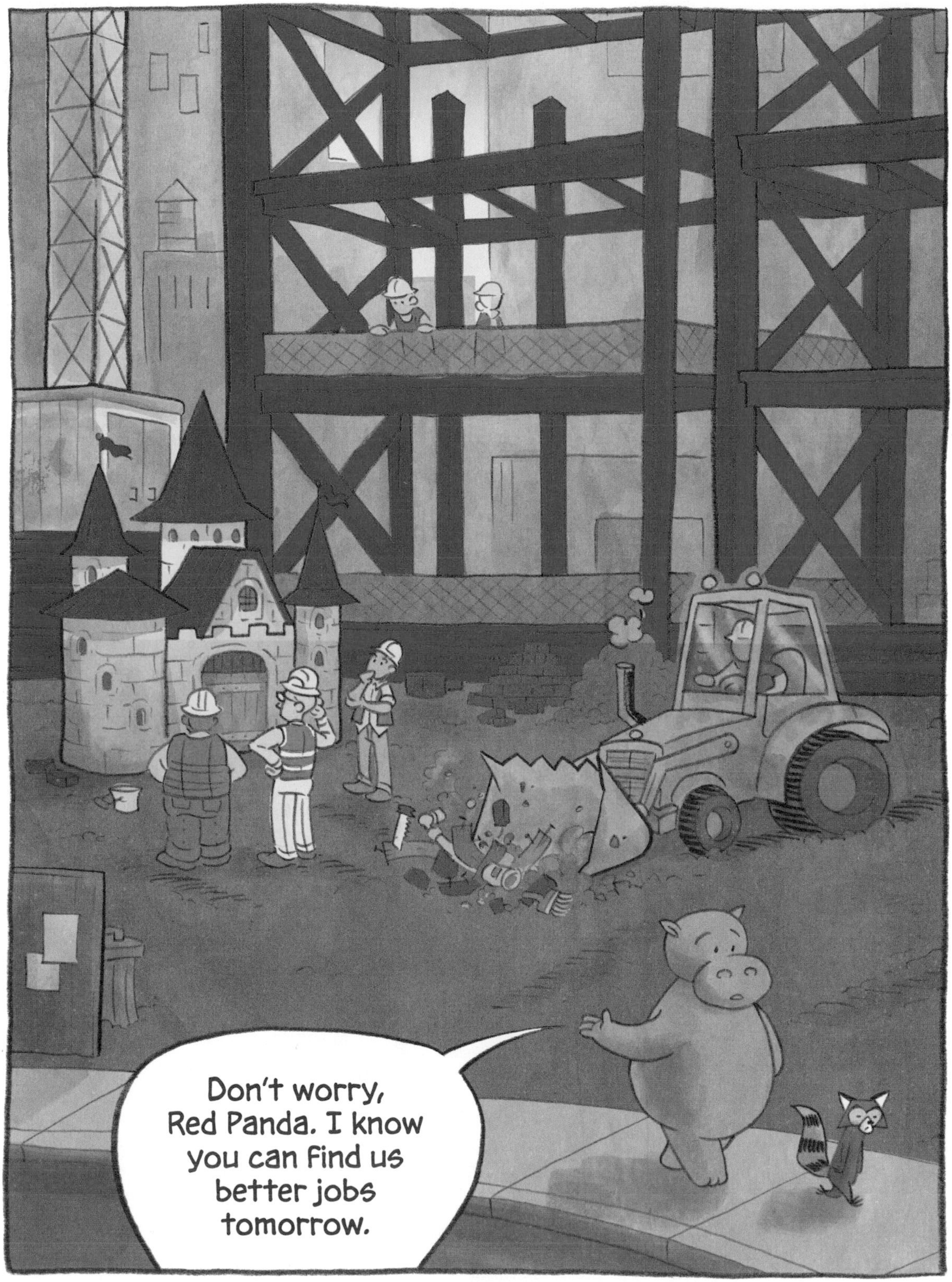
Don't worry, Red Panda. I know you can find us better jobs tomorrow.

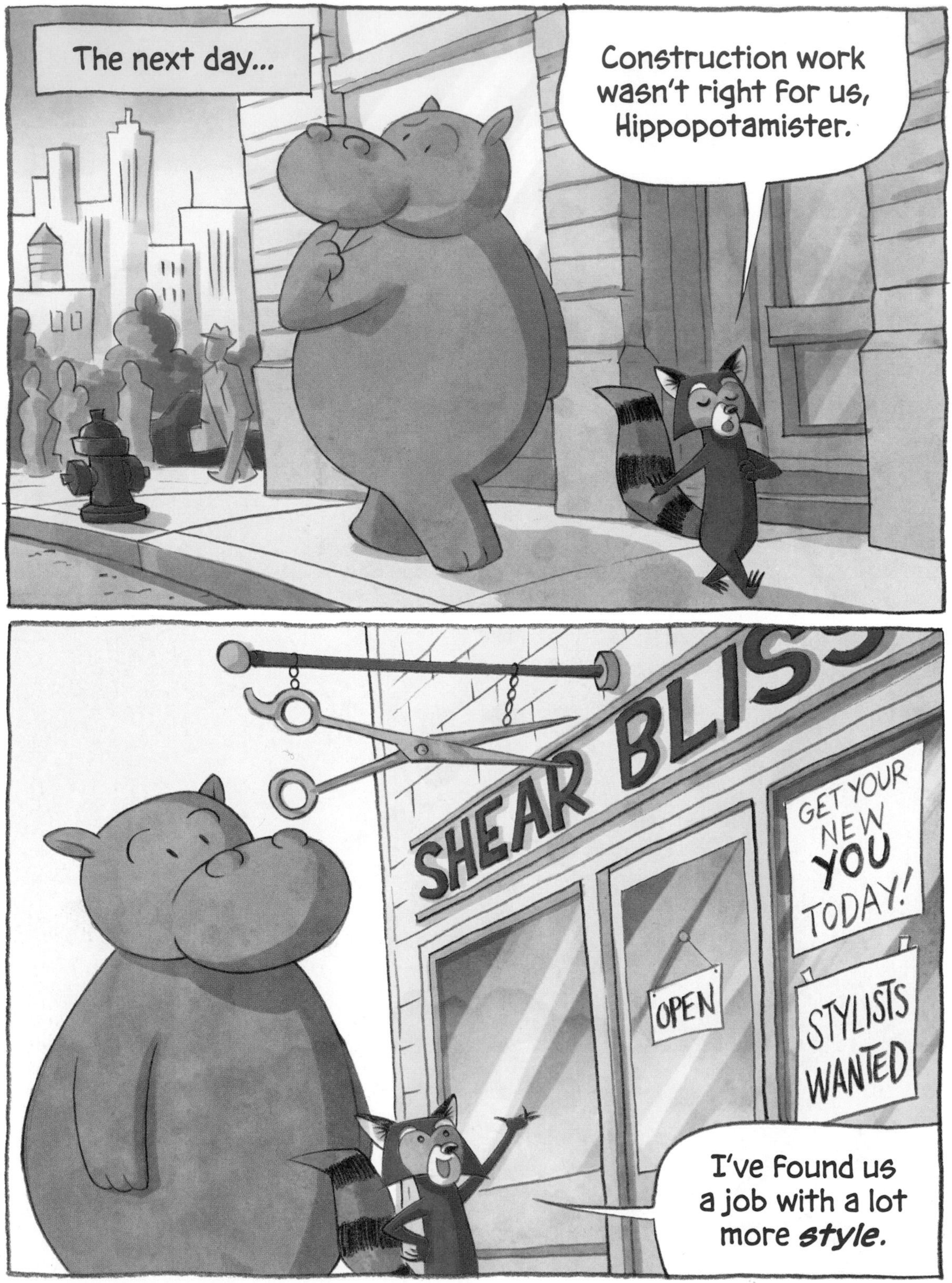
The next day...
Construction work wasn't right for us, Hippopotamister.
SHEAR BLISS
GET YOUR NEW YOU TODAY!
OPEN
STYLISTS WANTED
I've found us a job with a lot more *style.*

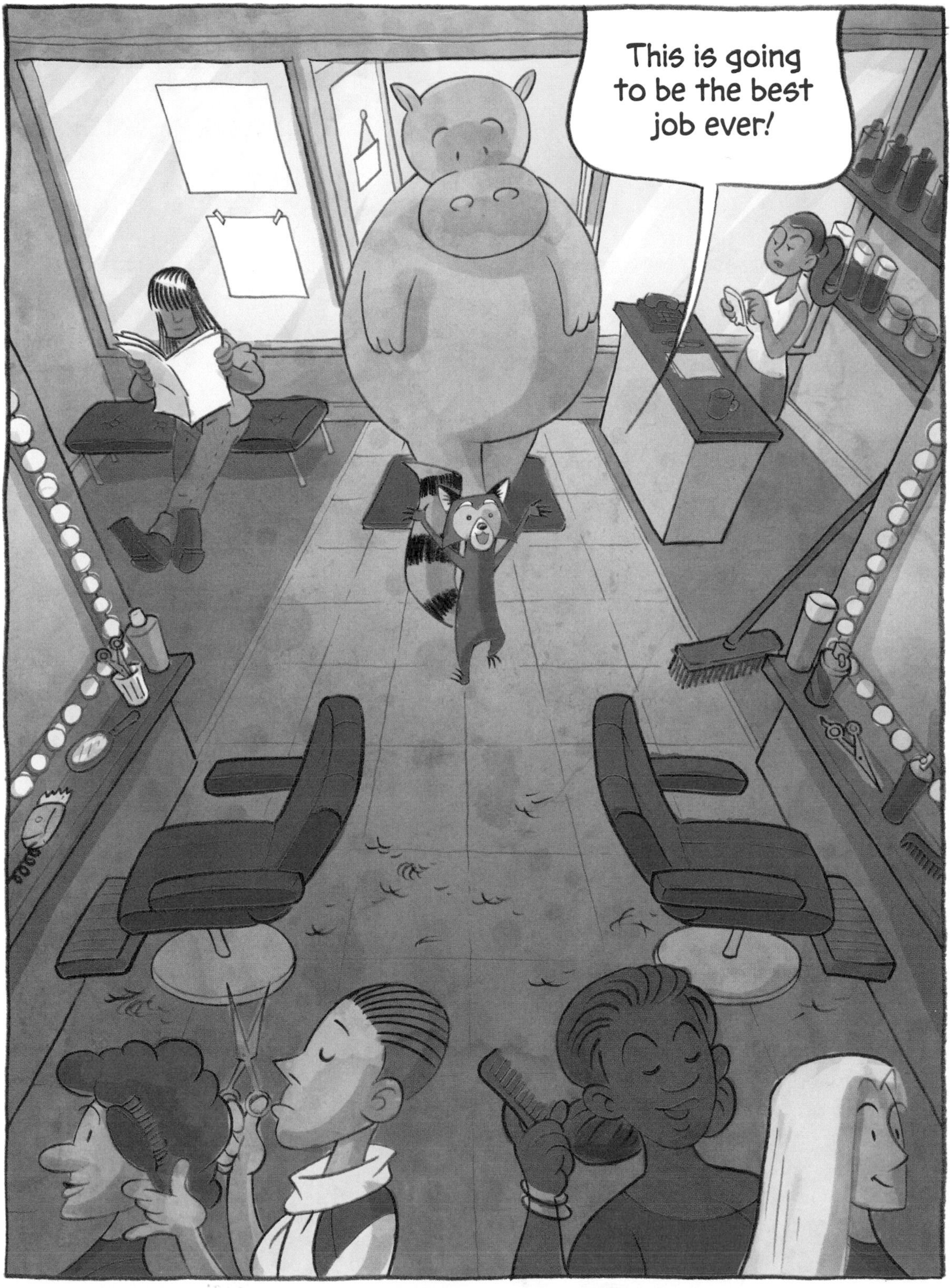
This is going to be the best job ever!

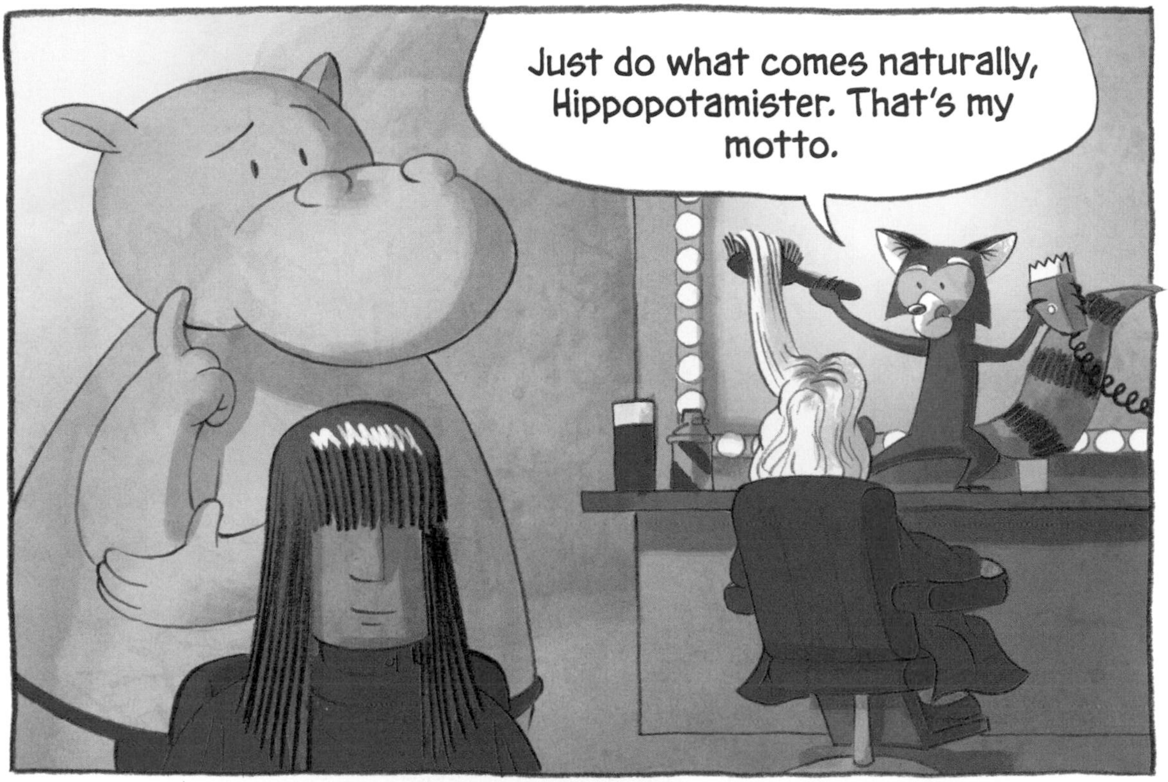
Just do what comes naturally, Hippopotamister. That's my motto.

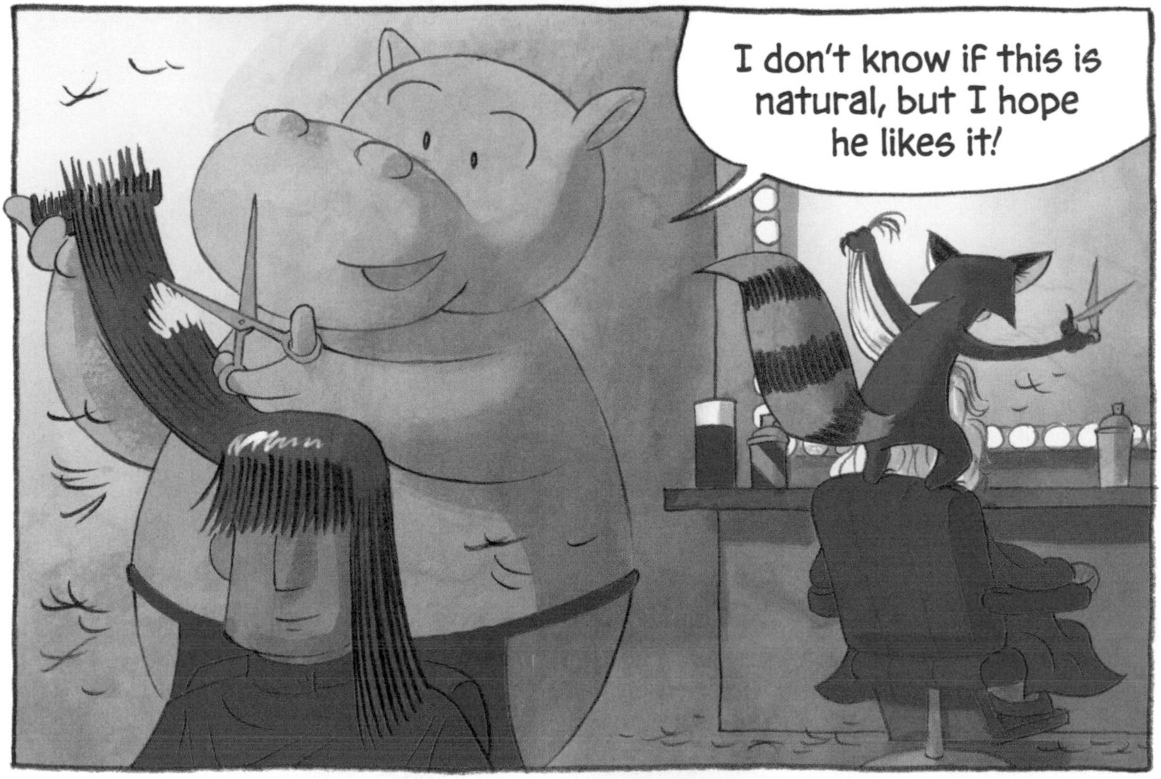
I don't know if this is natural, but I hope he likes it!

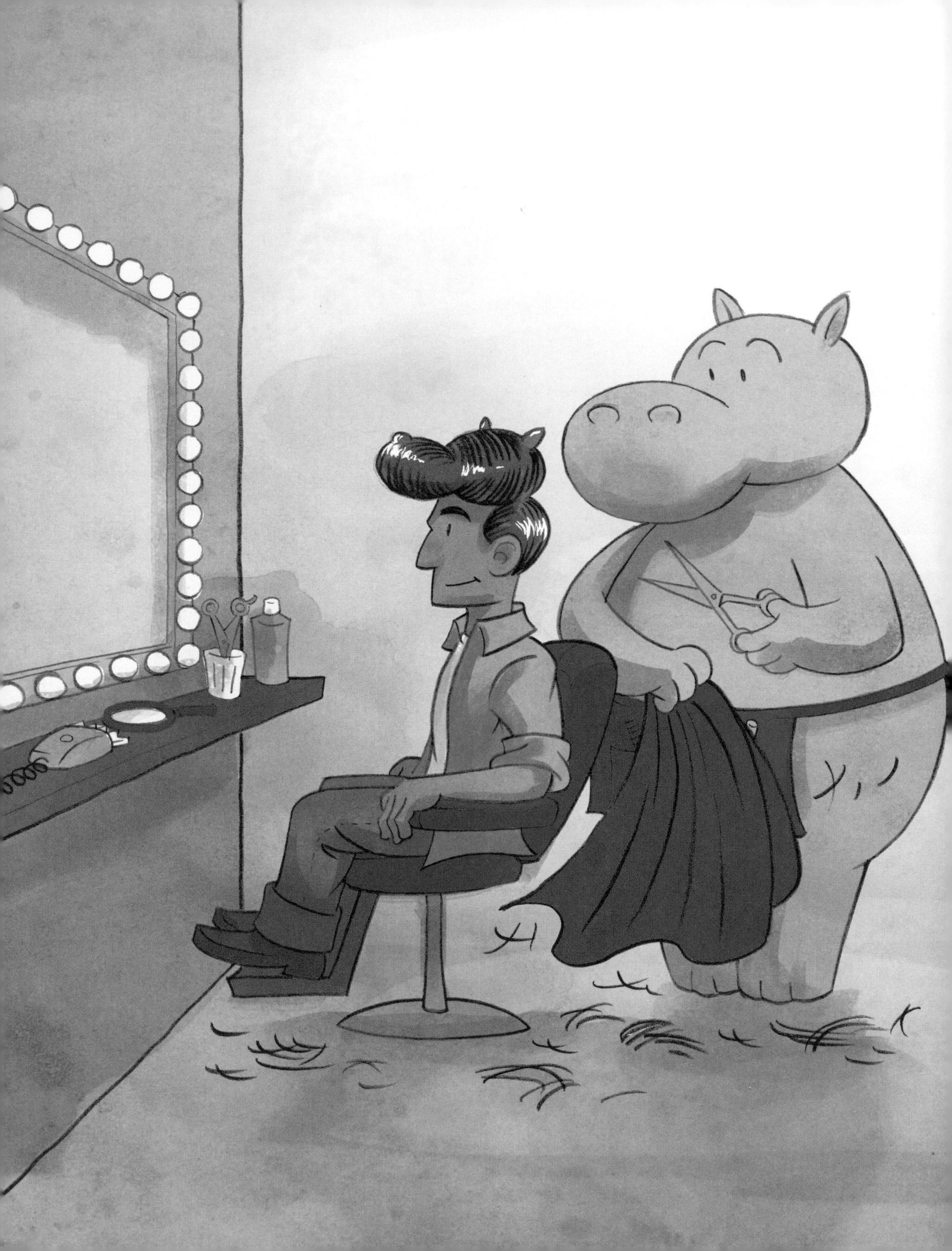

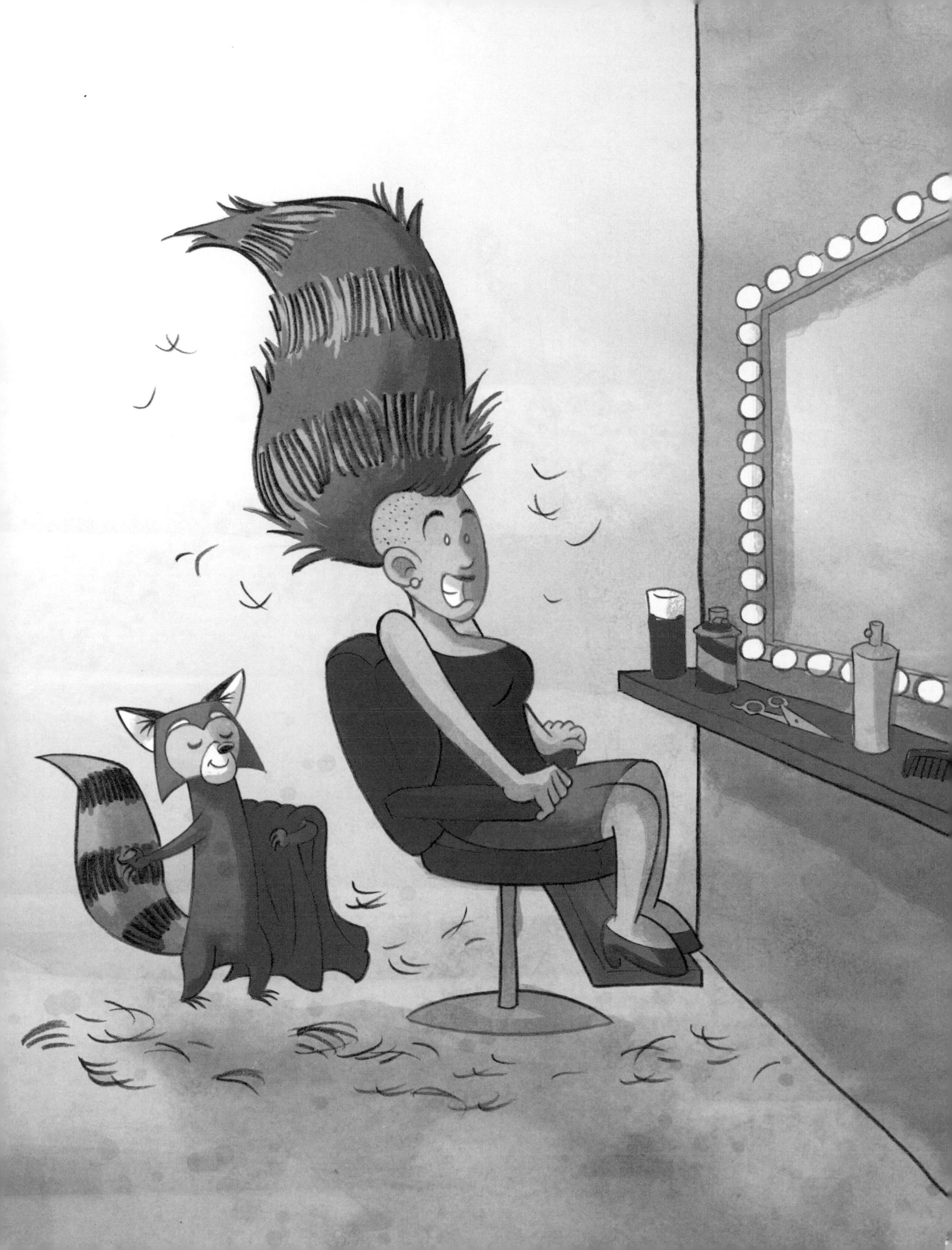

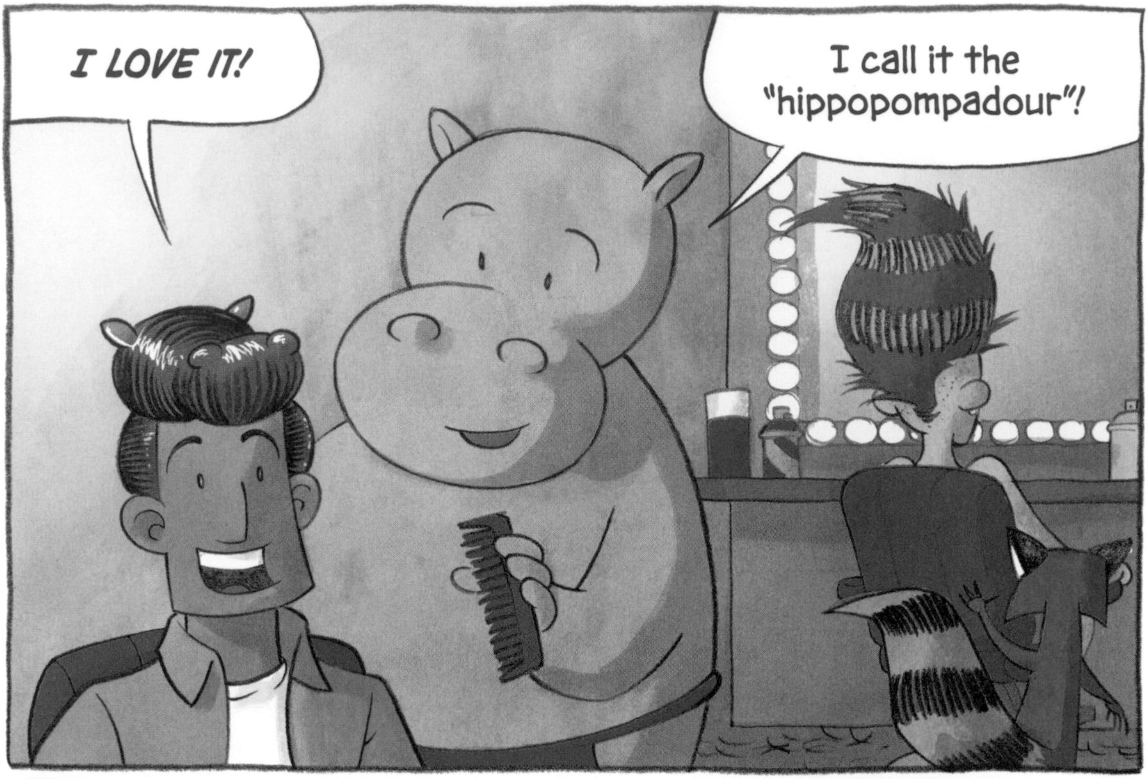
I LOVE IT!
I call it the "hippopompadour"!

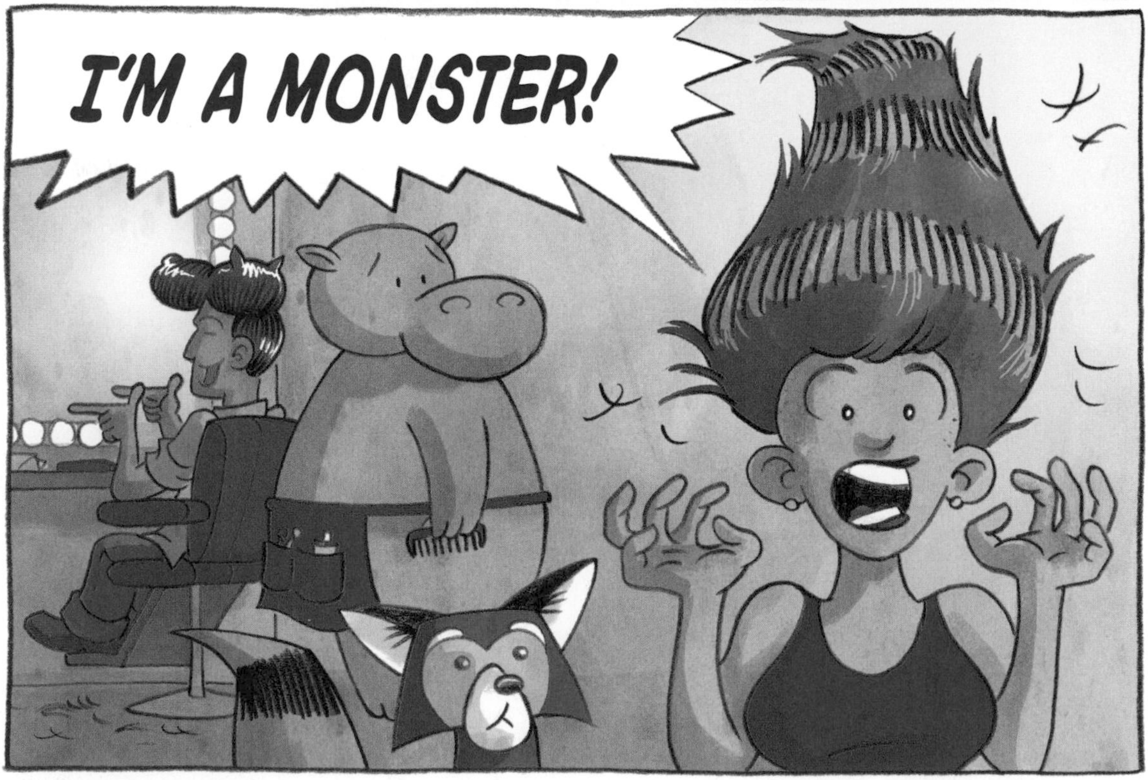
I'M A MONSTER!

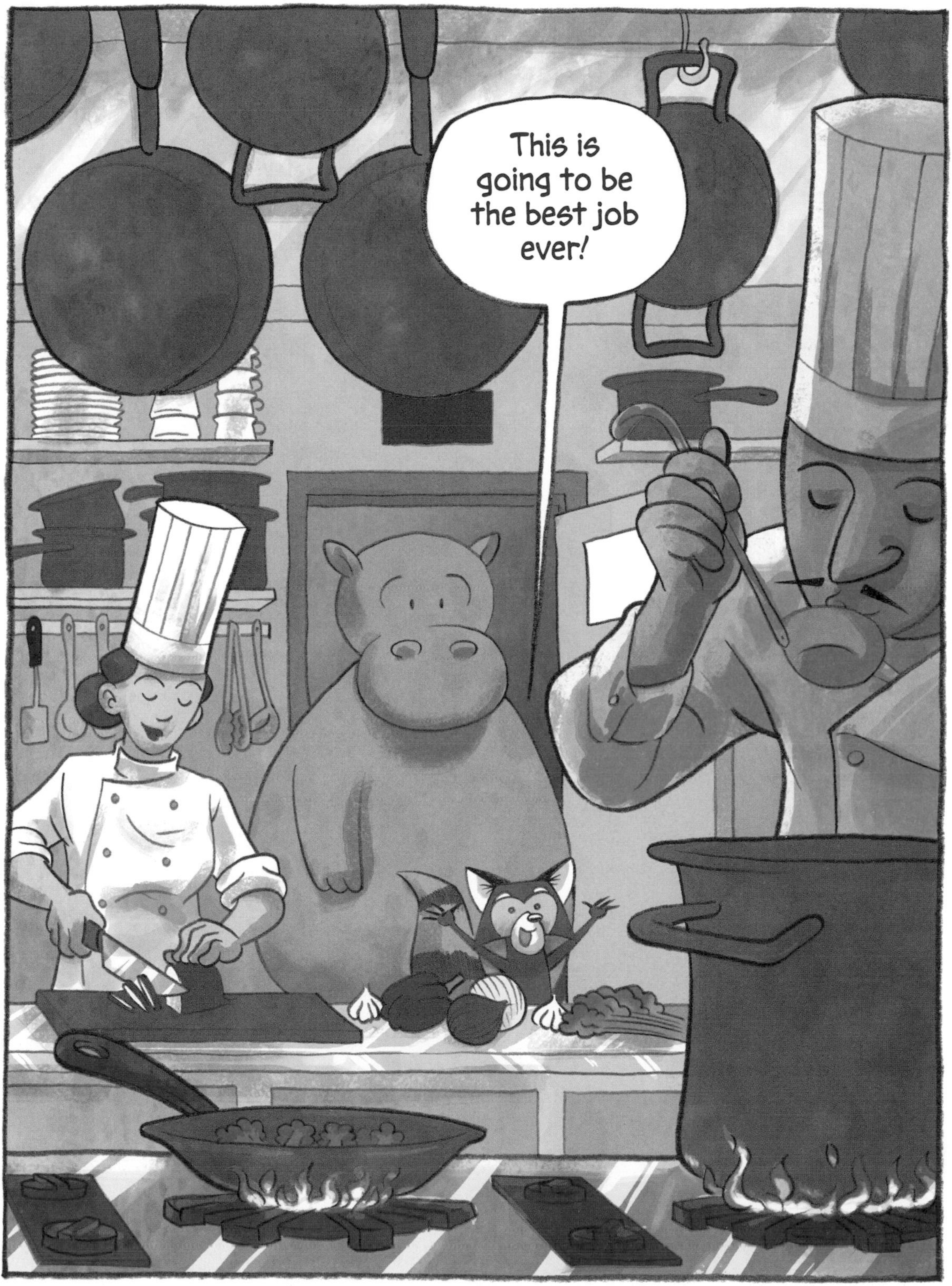
This is going to be the best job ever!

26

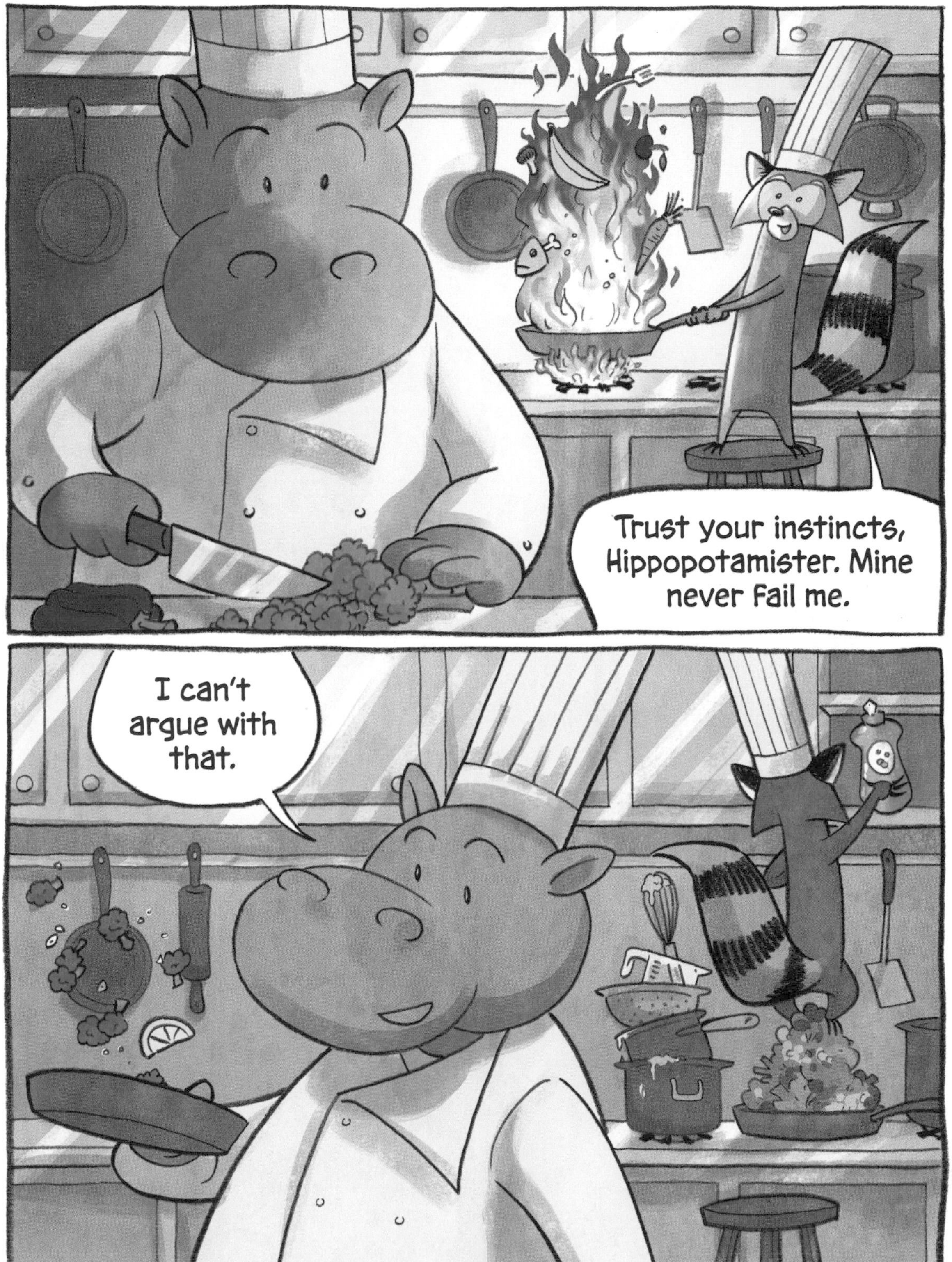
Trust your instincts, Hippopotamister. Mine never fail me.
I can't argue with that.

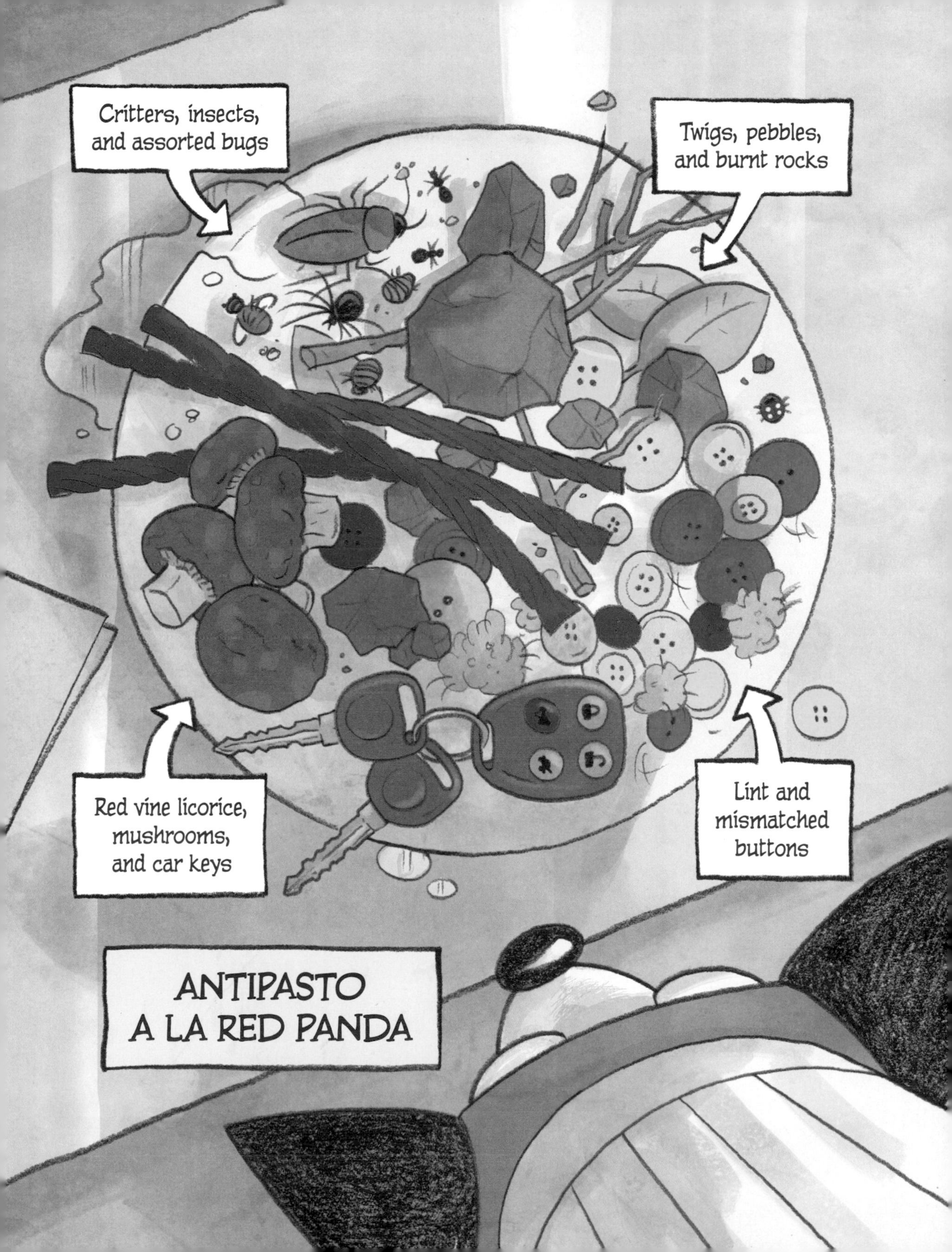
Critters, insects, and assorted bugs
Twigs, pebbles, and burnt rocks
Red vine licorice, mushrooms, and car keys
Lint and mismatched buttons
ANTIPASTO A LA RED PANDA

30

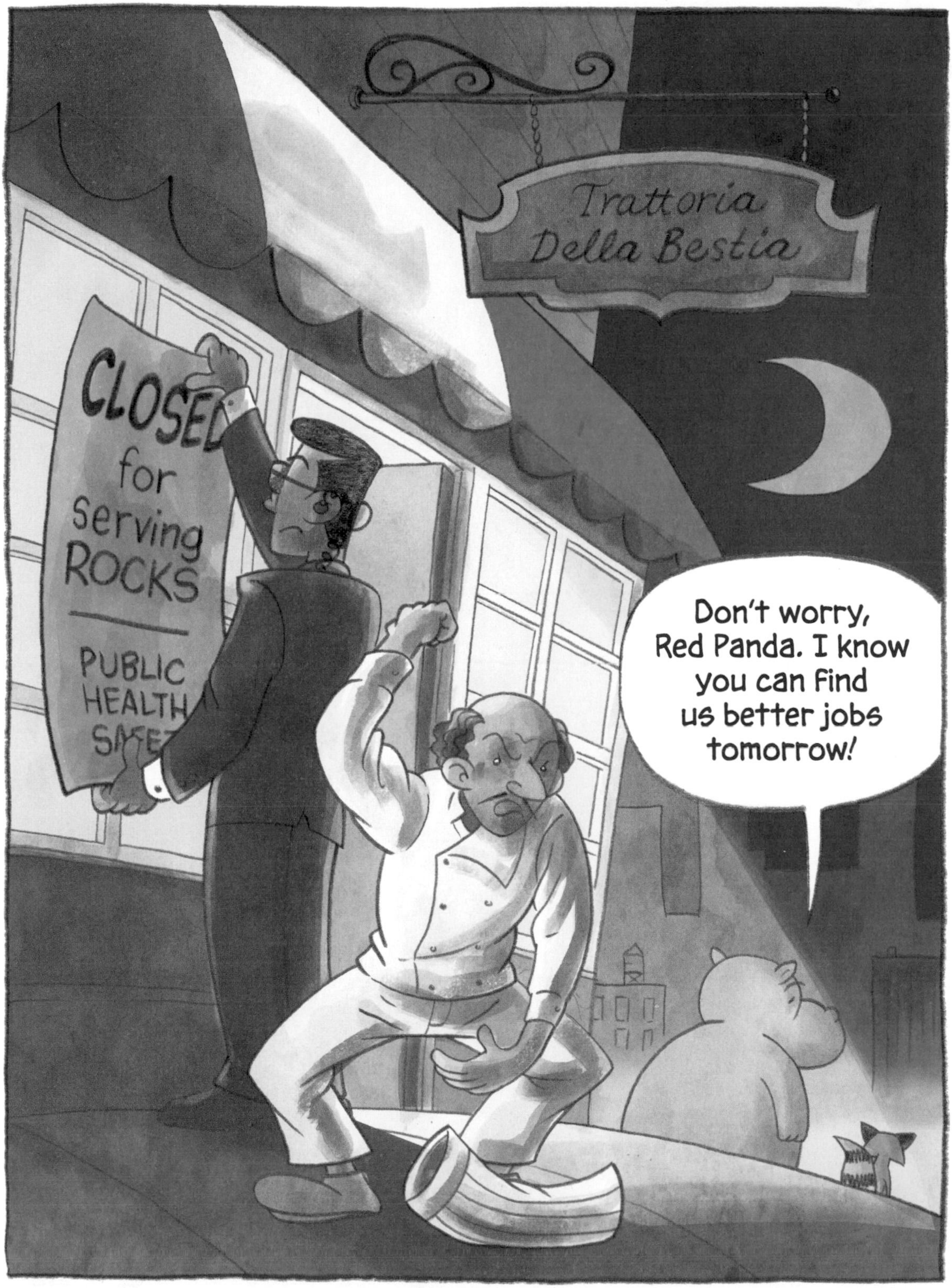
Trattoria Della Bestia
CLOSED for serving ROCKS
PUBLIC HEALTH
Don't worry, Red Panda. I know you can find us better jobs tomorrow!

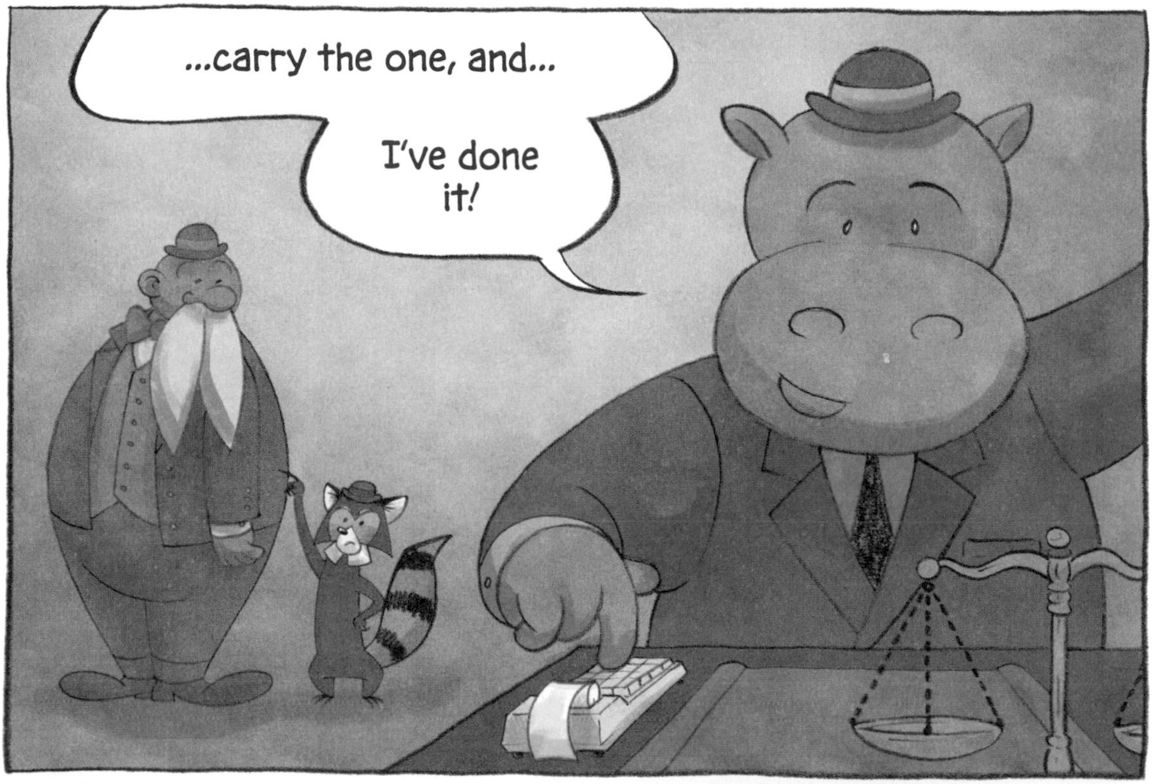
...carry the one, and...
I've done it!

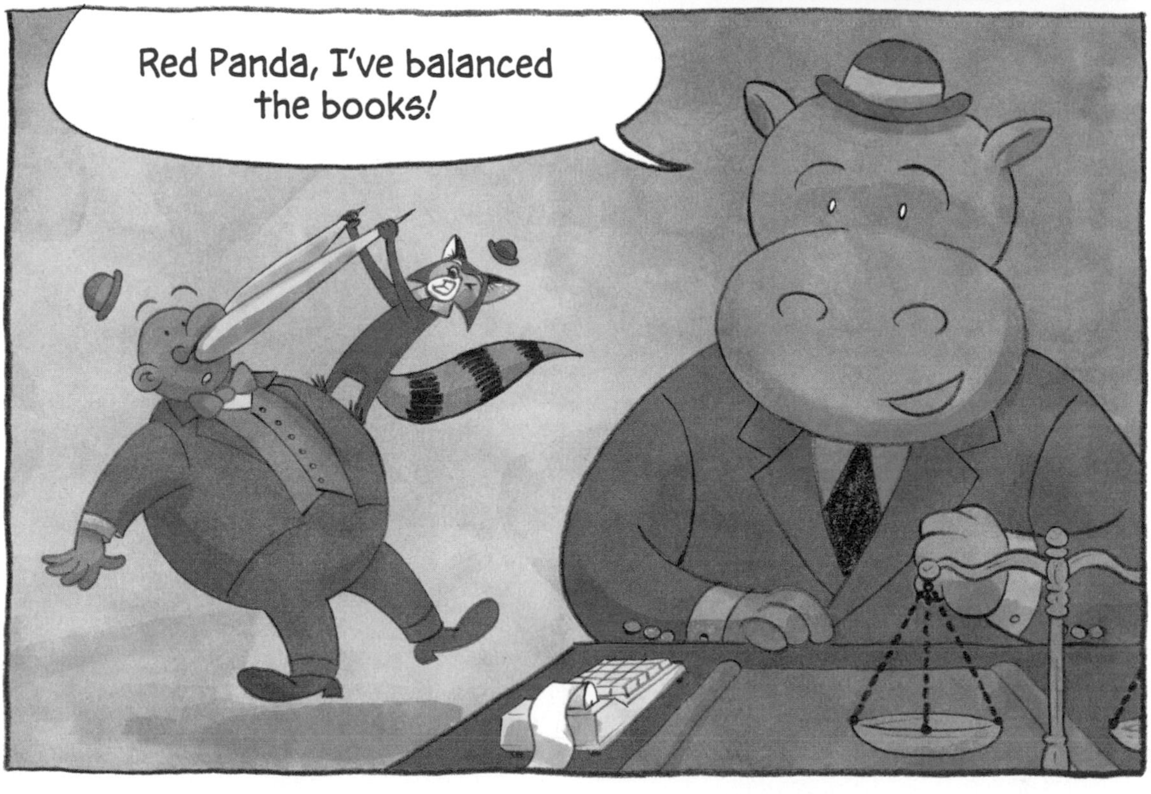
Red Panda, I've balanced the books!

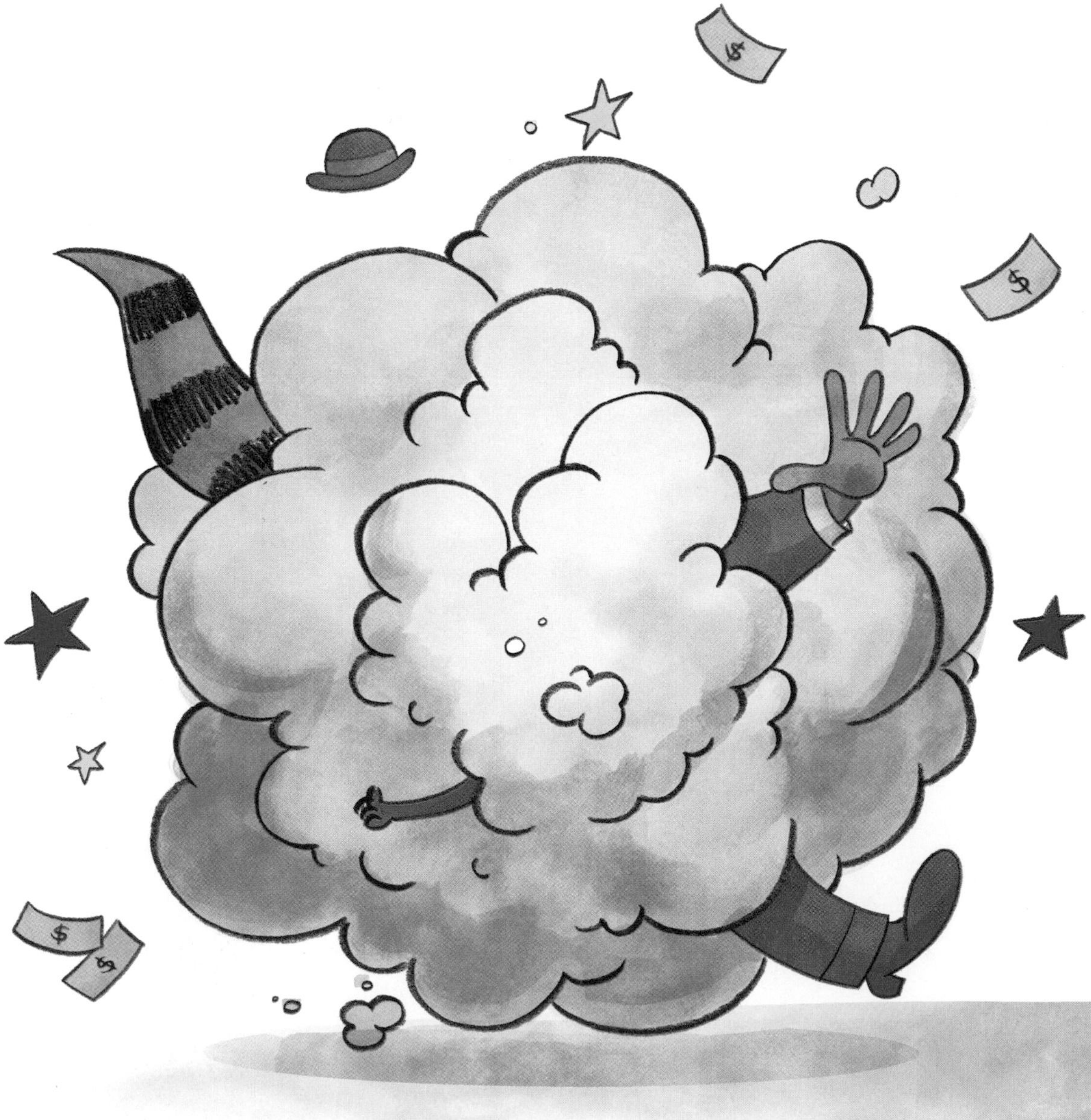

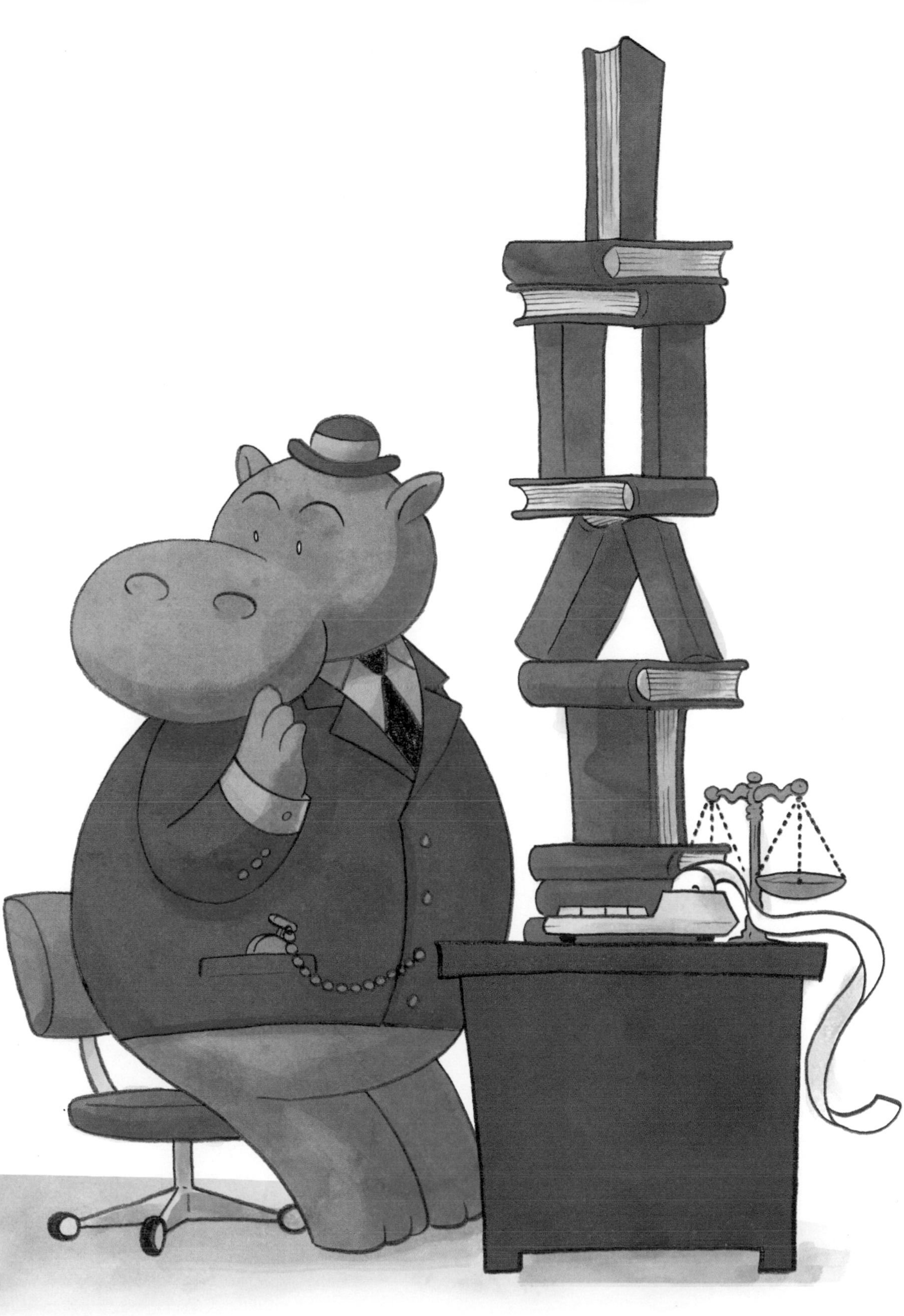

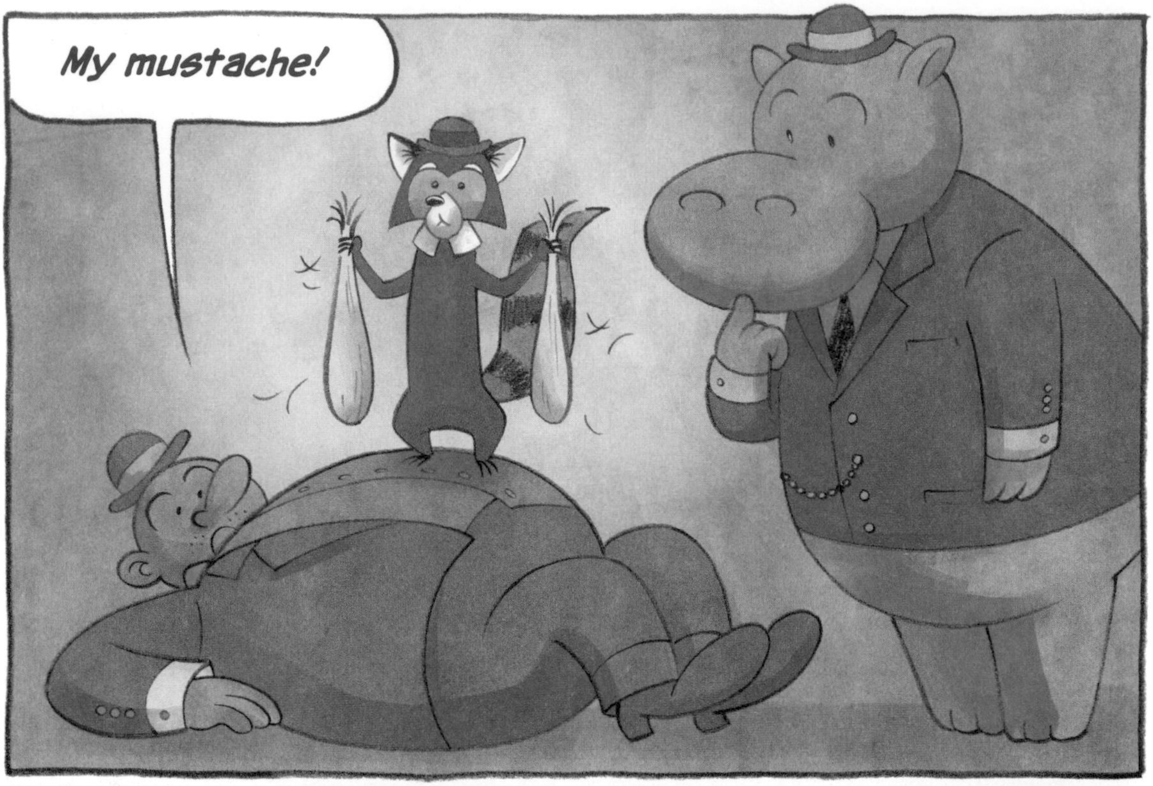
My mustache!

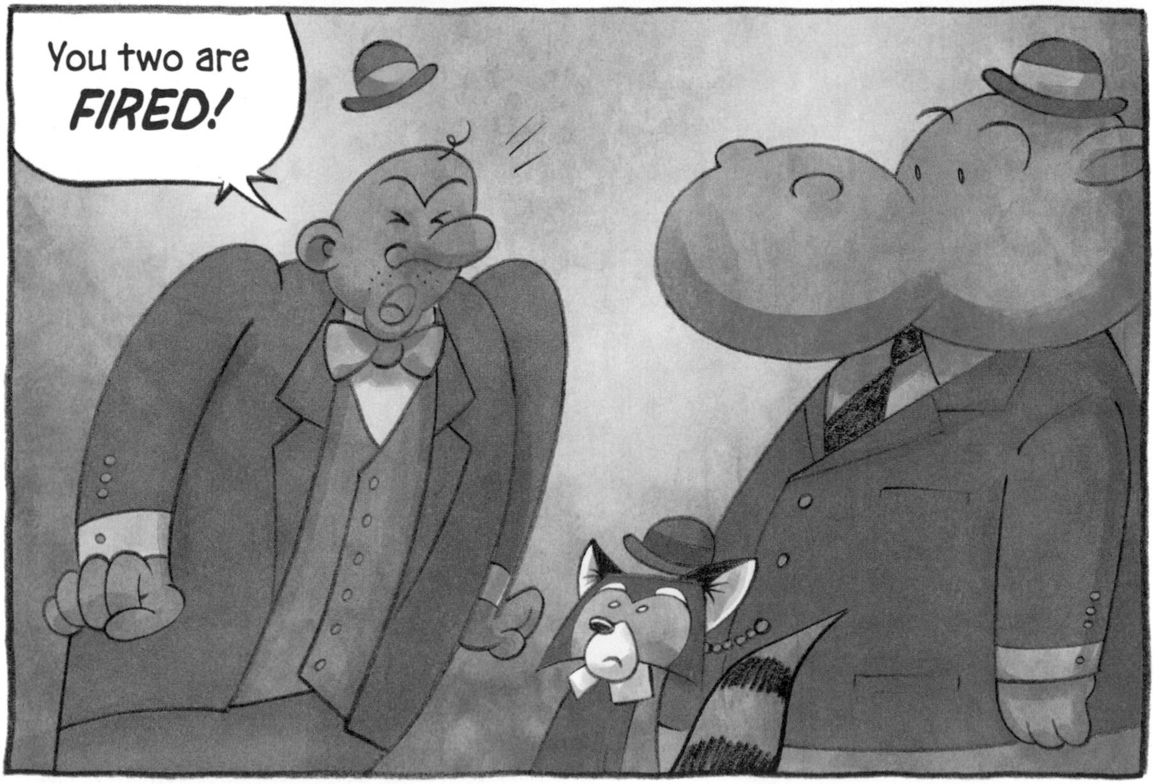
You two are **FIRED!**

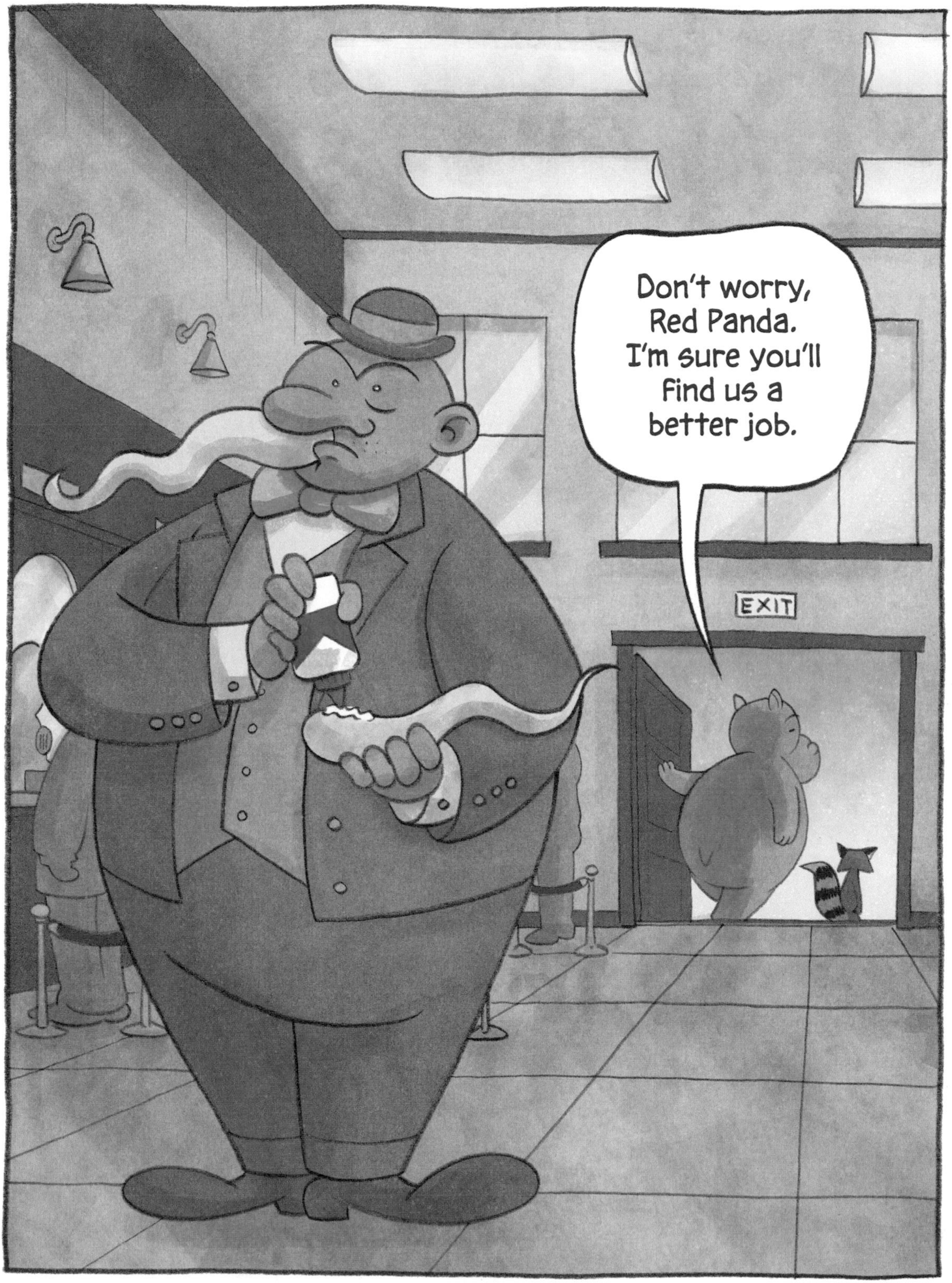
Don't worry, Red Panda. I'm sure you'll find us a better job.
EXIT

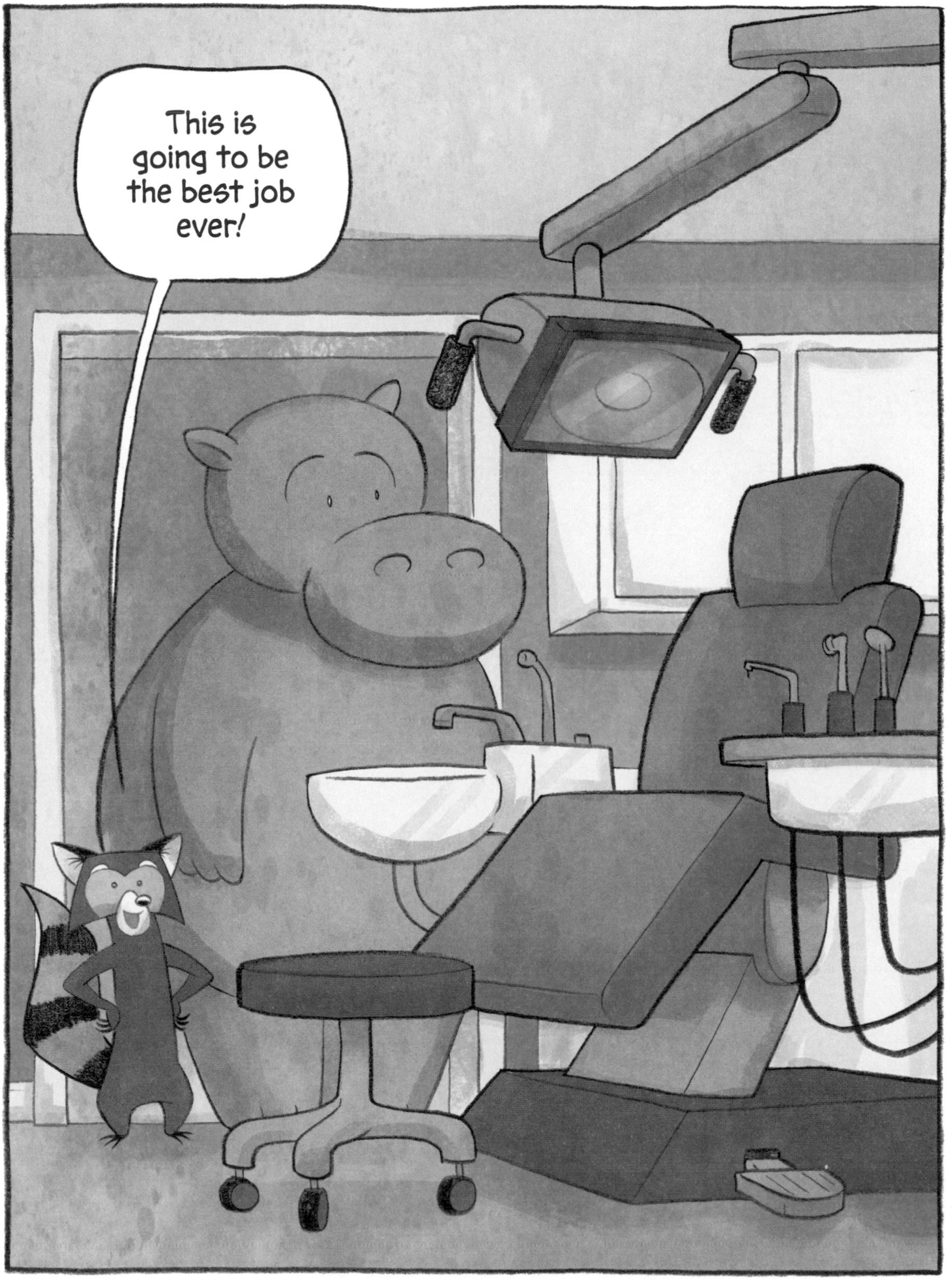
This is going to be the best job ever!

42

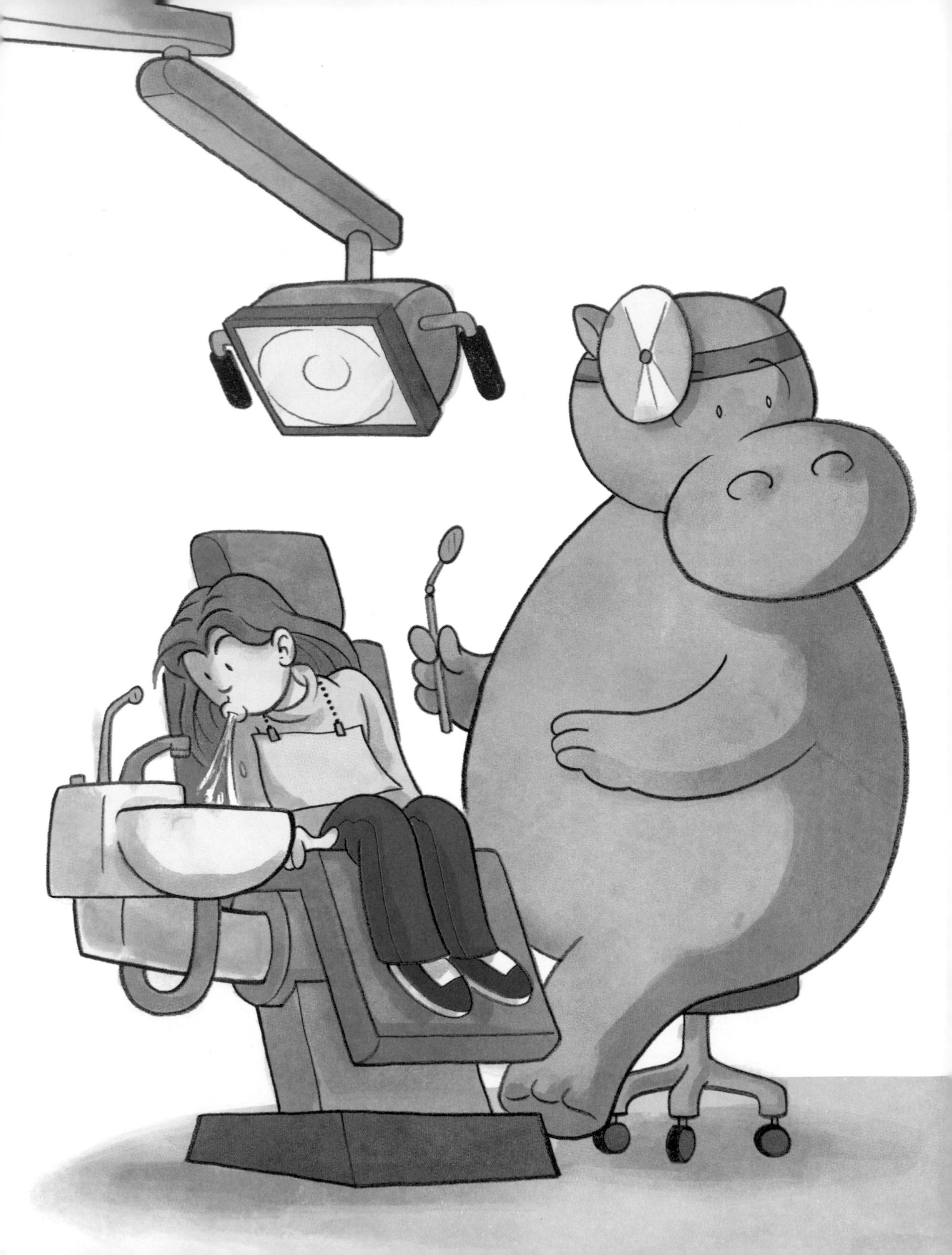

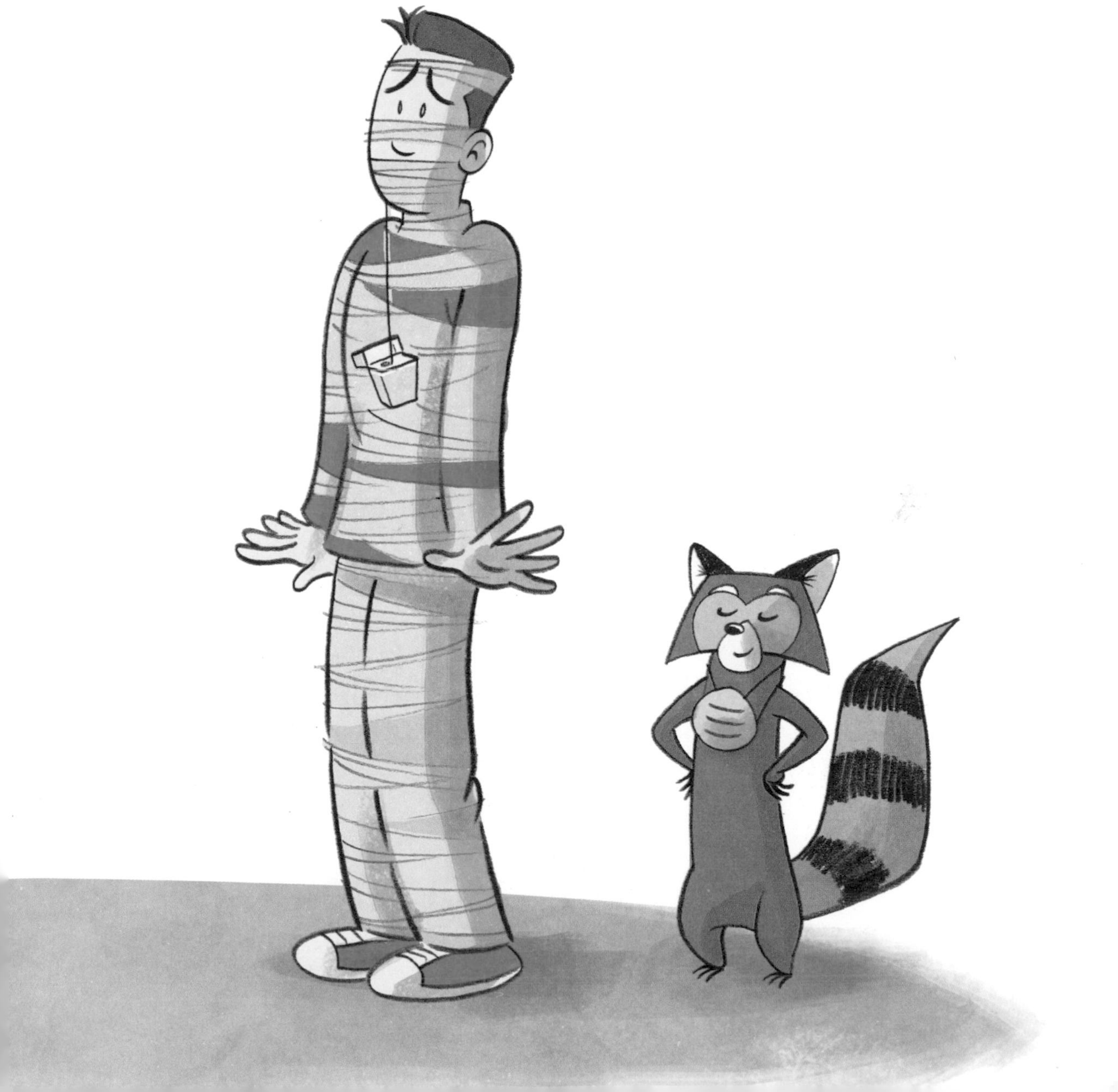

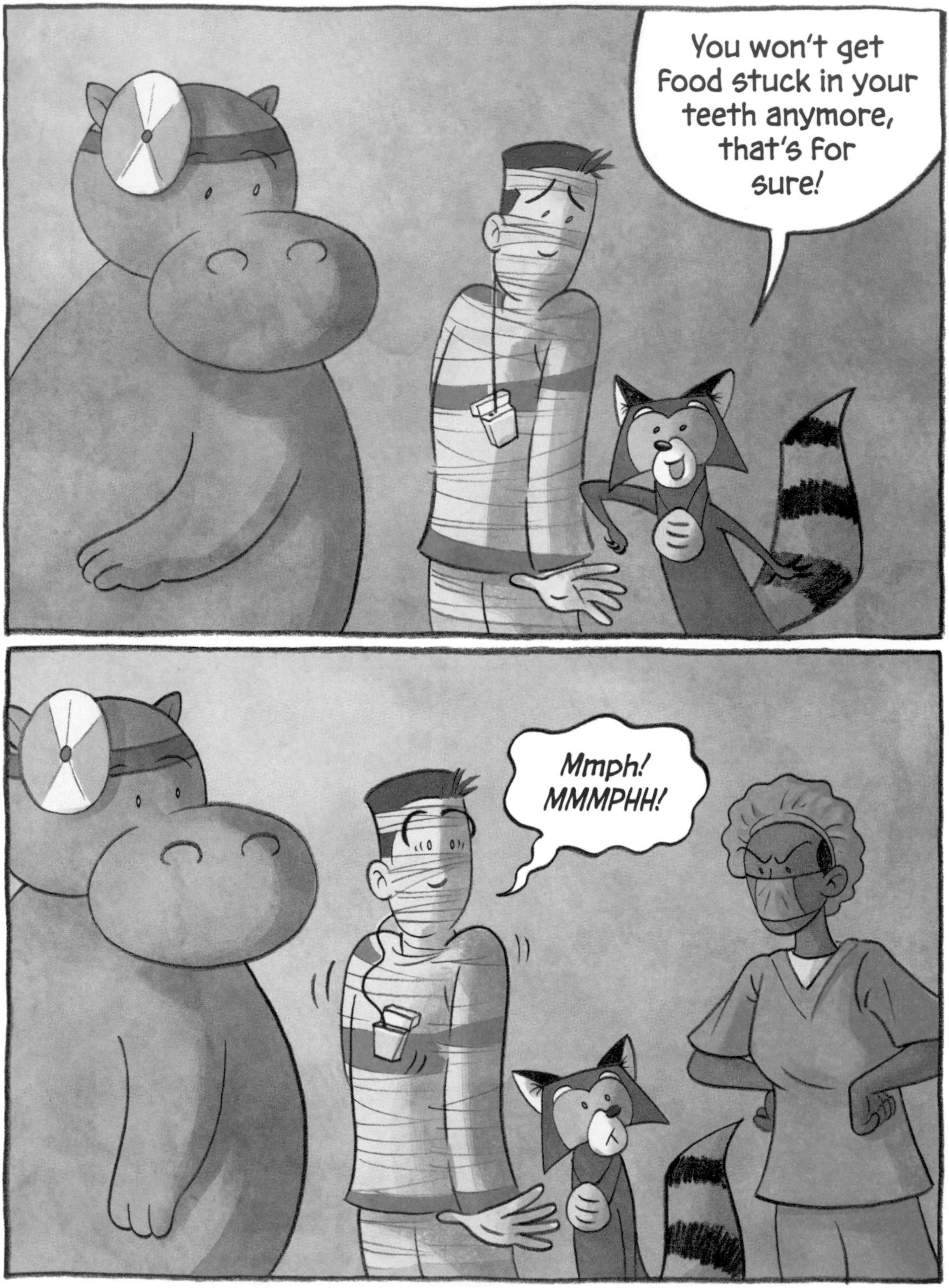
You won't get food stuck in your teeth anymore, that's for sure!
Mmph! MMMPHH!

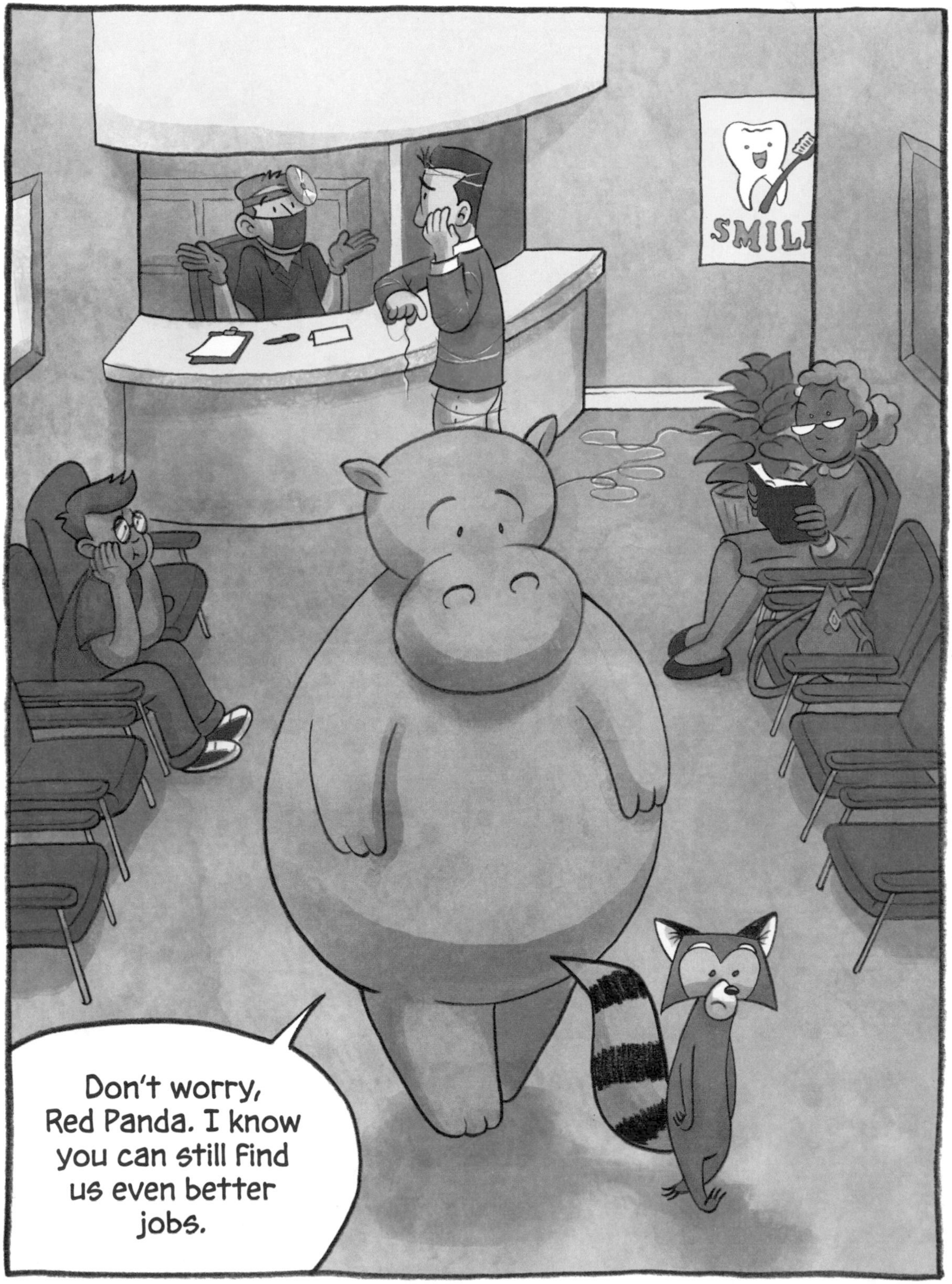
SMILE
Don't worry, Red Panda. I know you can still find us even better jobs.

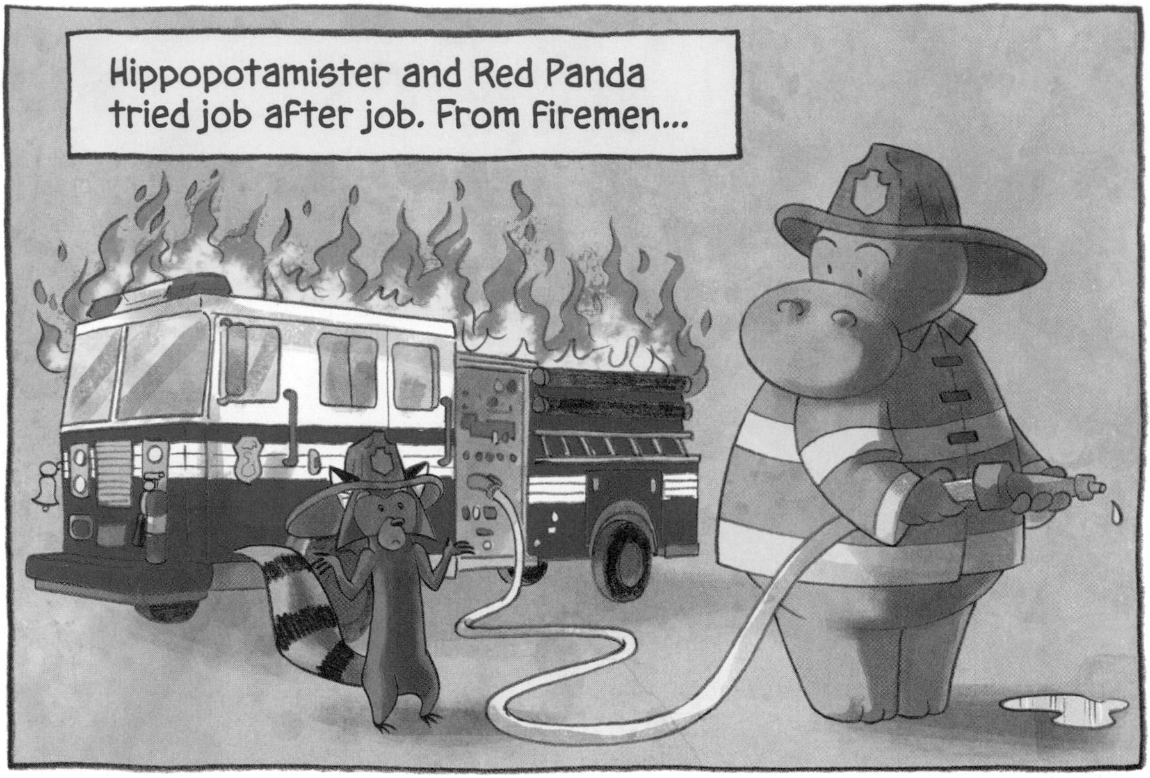
Hippopotamister and Red Panda tried job after job. From firemen...

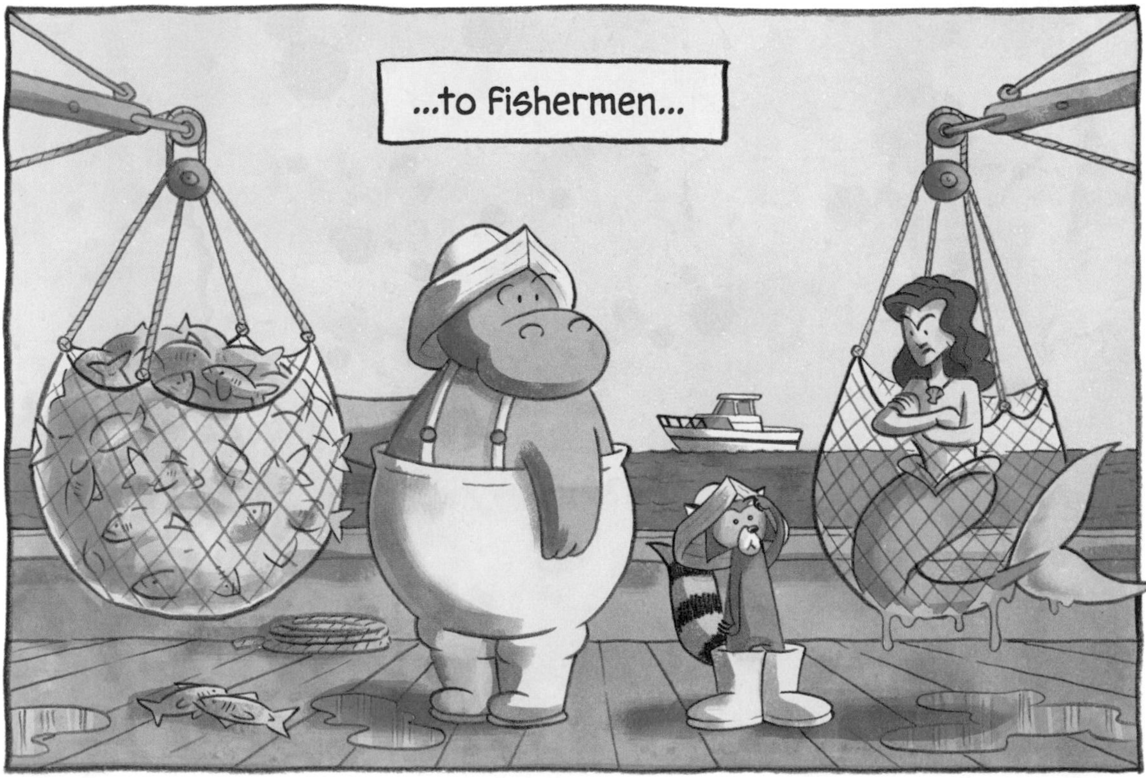
...to fishermen...

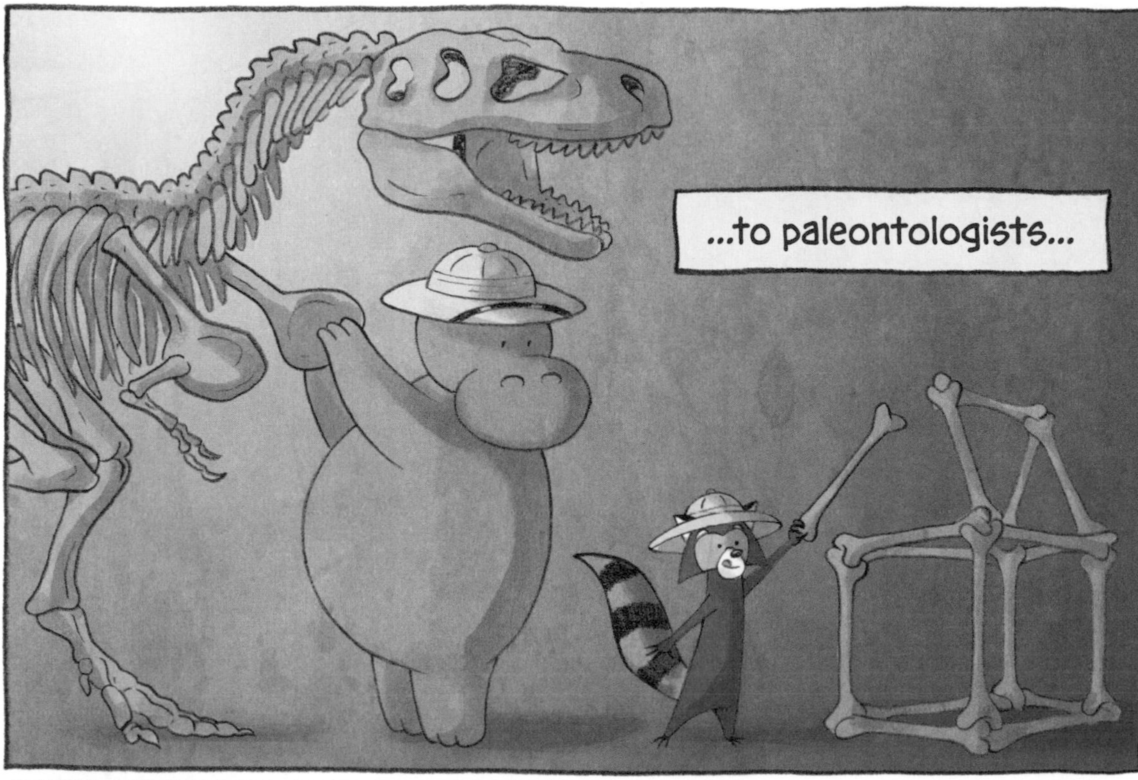
...to paleontologists...

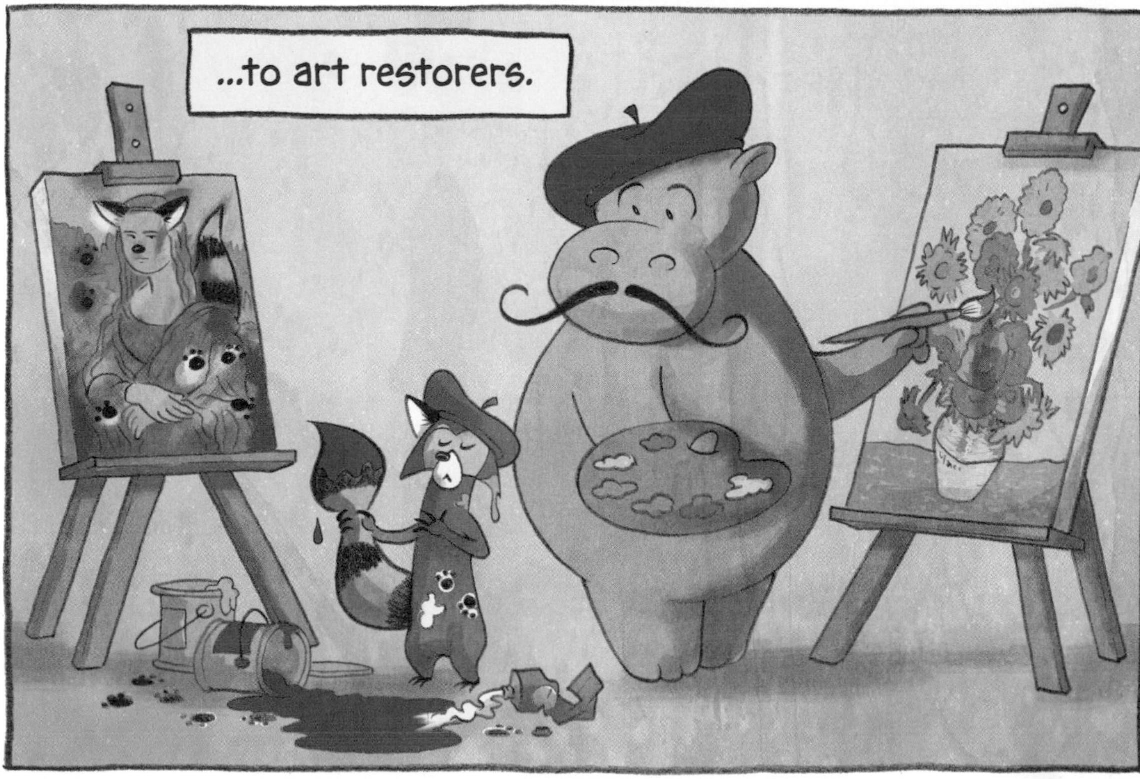
...to art restorers.

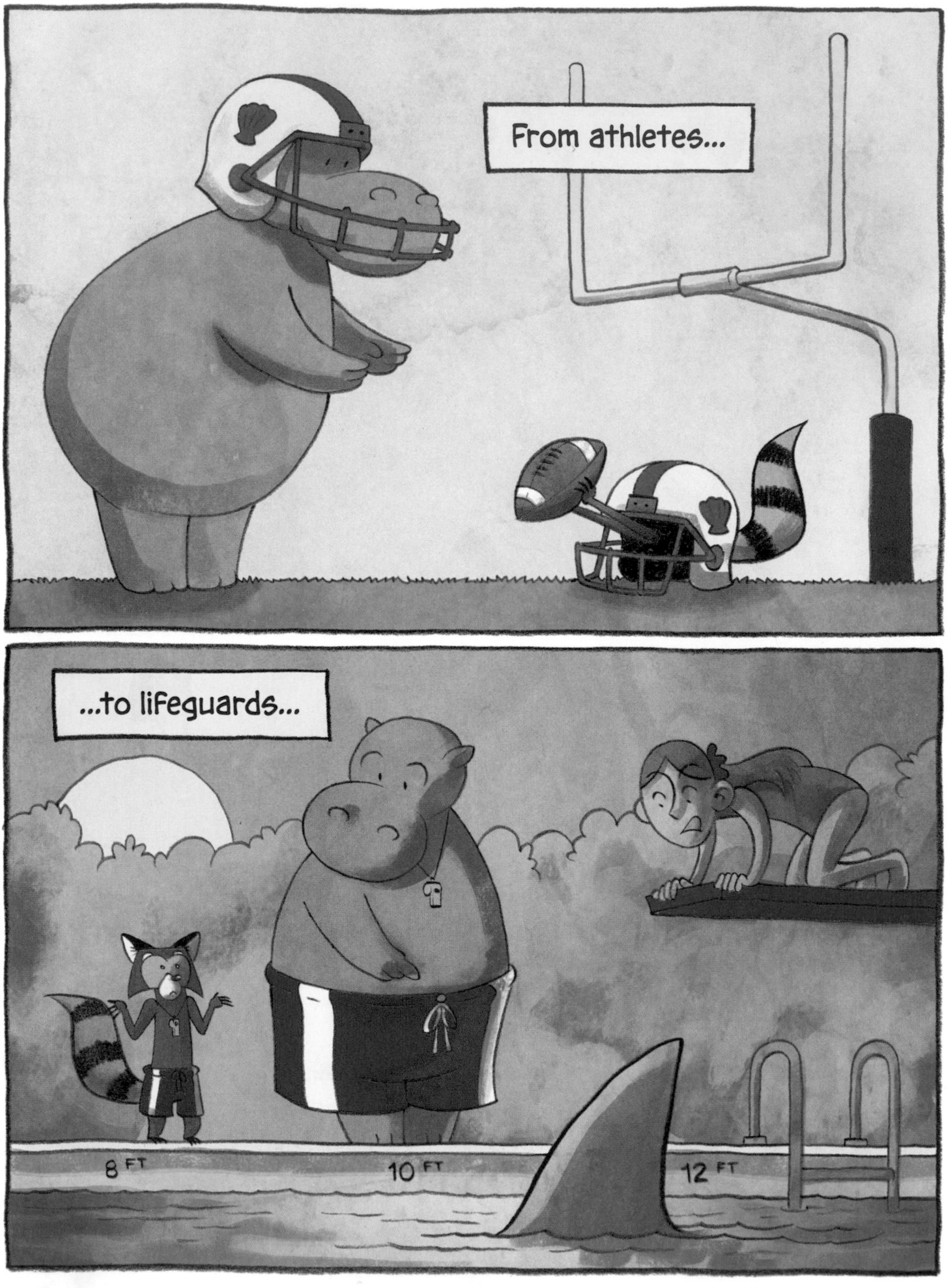
From athletes...
...to lifeguards...
8 FT
10 FT
12 FT

51

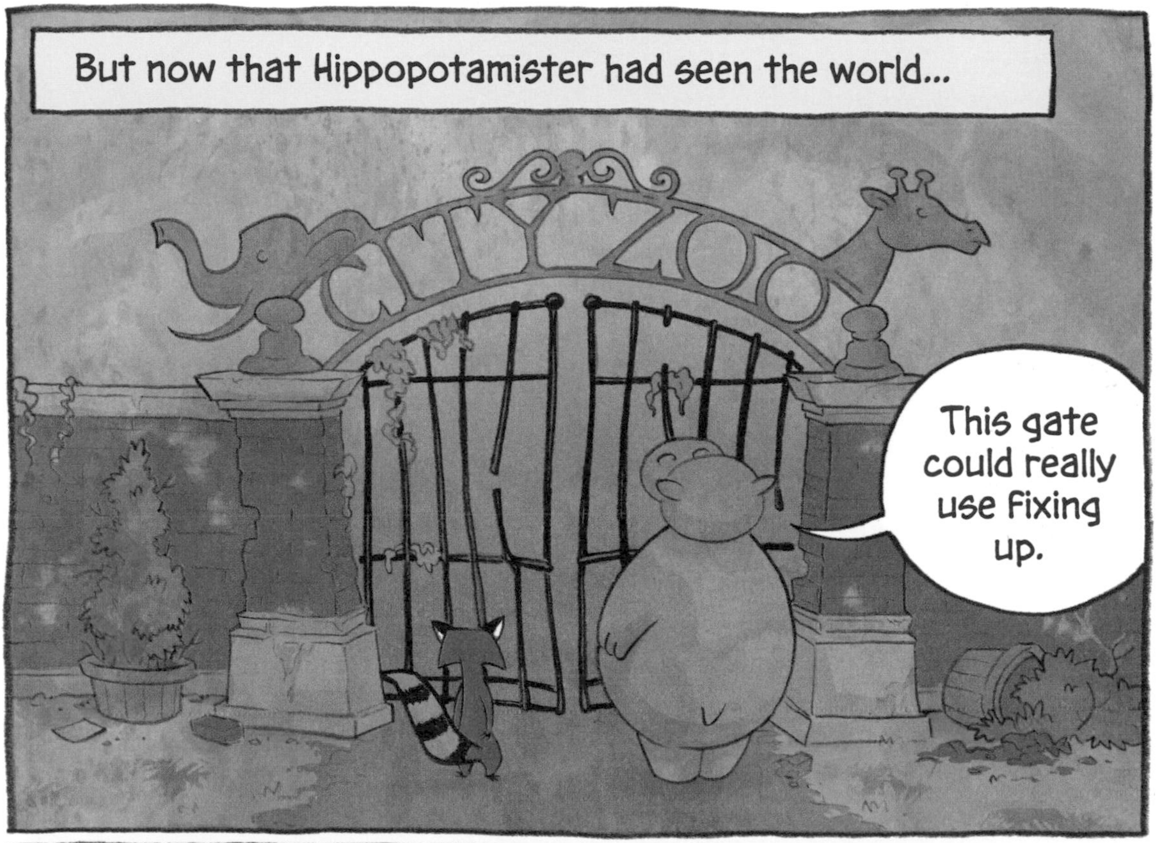
But now that Hippopotamister had seen the world...
CITY ZOO
This gate could really use fixing up.

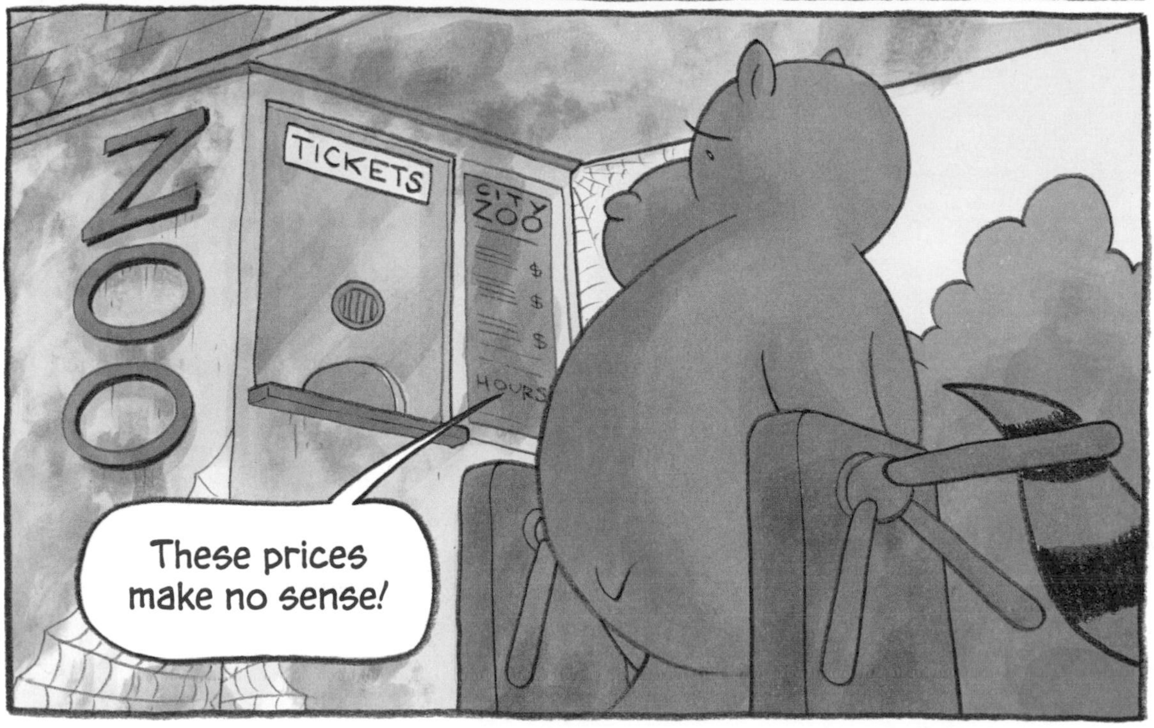
ZOO
TICKETS
CITY ZOO
$
$
$
HOURS
These prices make no sense!

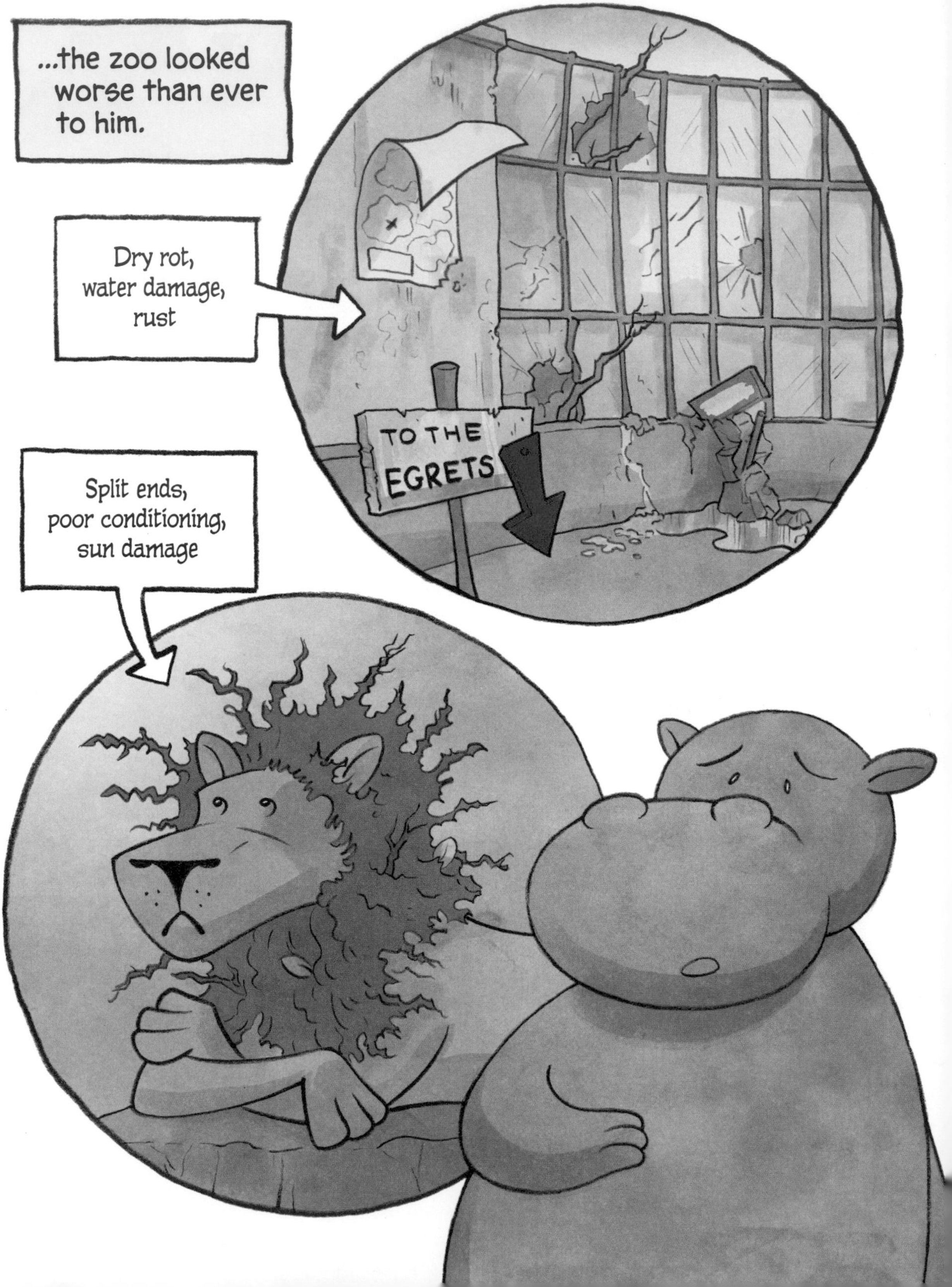
...the zoo looked worse than ever to him.
Dry rot, water damage, rust
TO THE EGRETS
Split ends, poor conditioning, sun damage

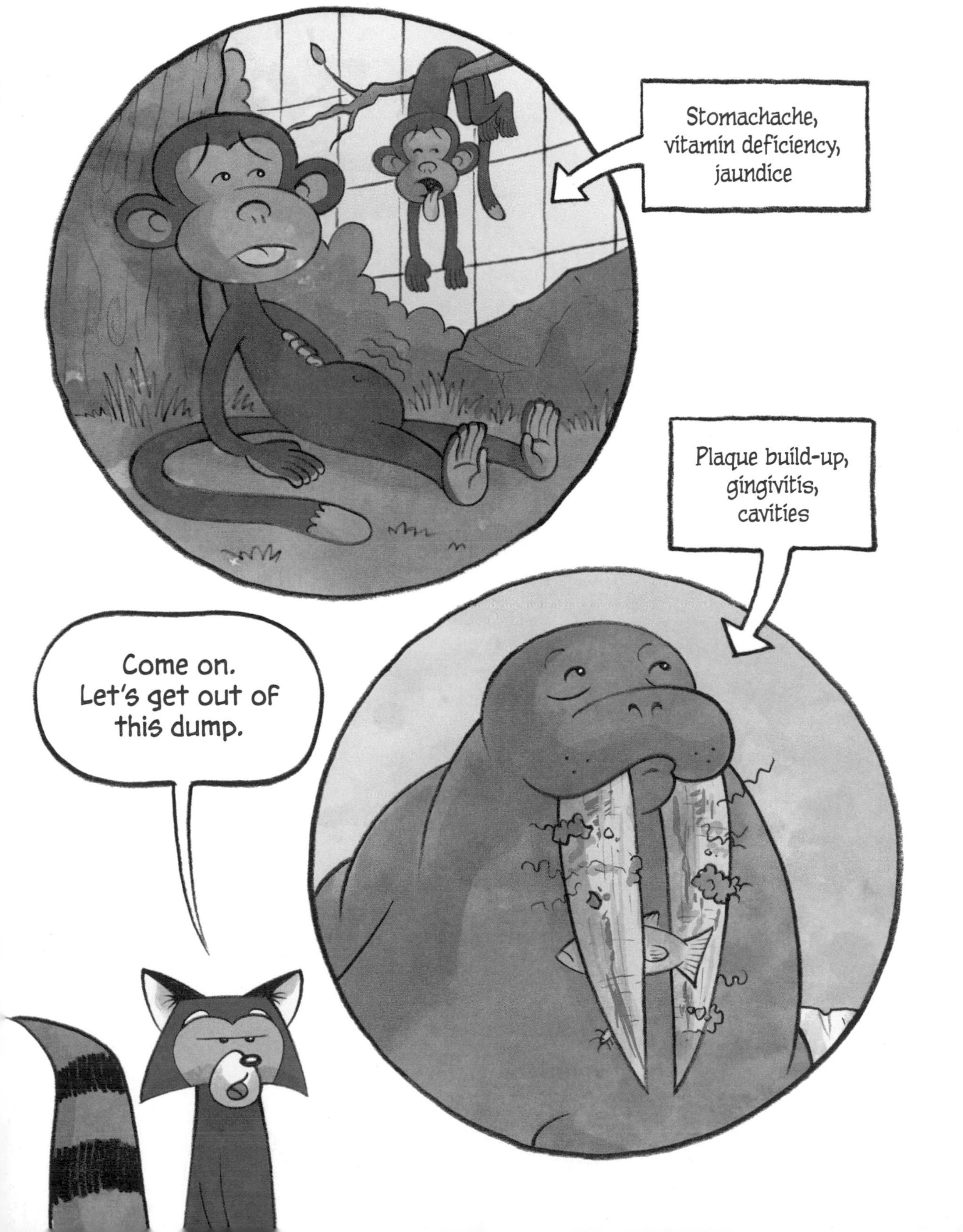
Stomachache, vitamin deficiency, jaundice
Plaque build-up, gingivitis, cavities
Come on. Let's get out of this dump.

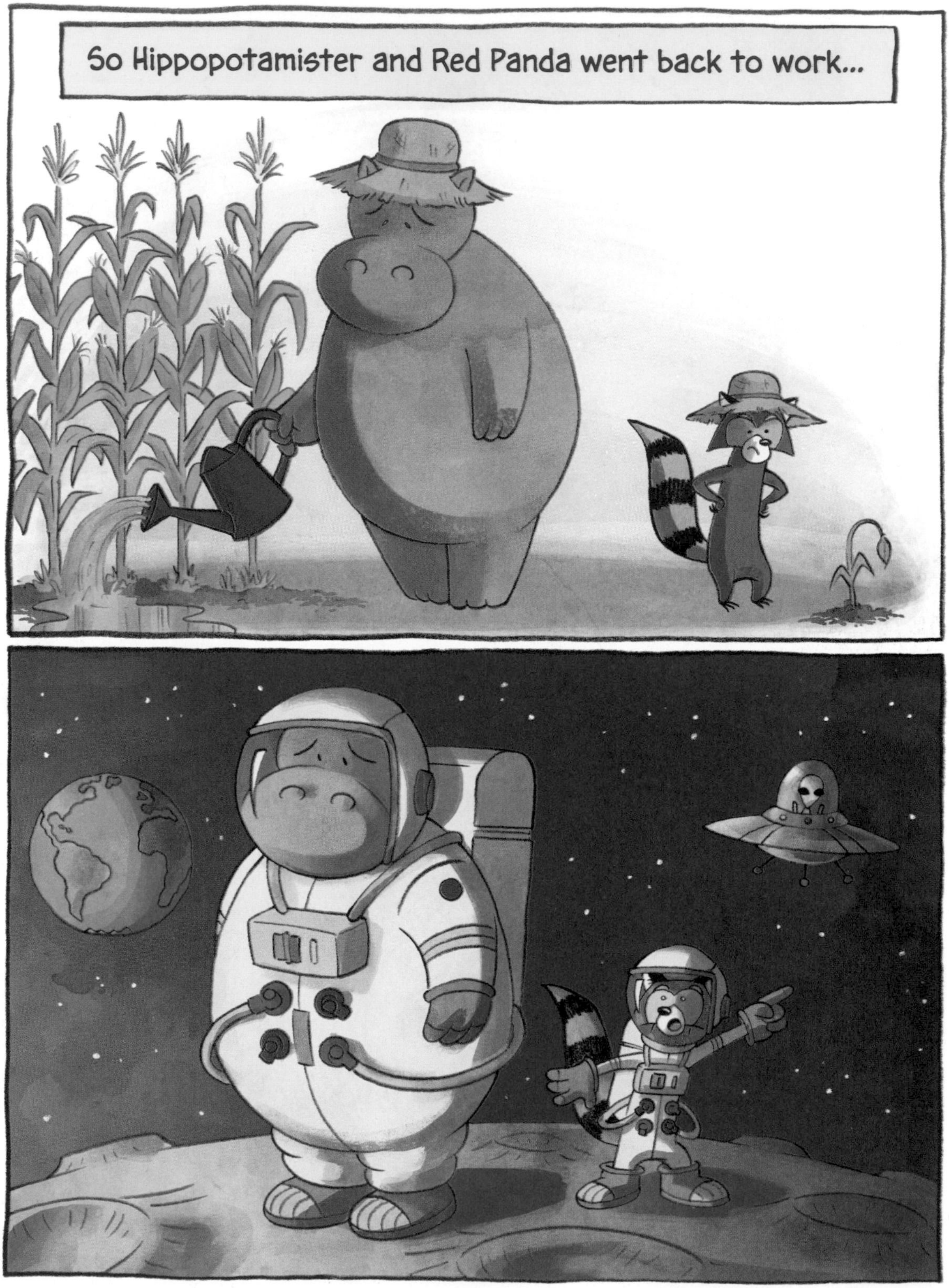
So Hippopotamister and Red Panda went back to work...

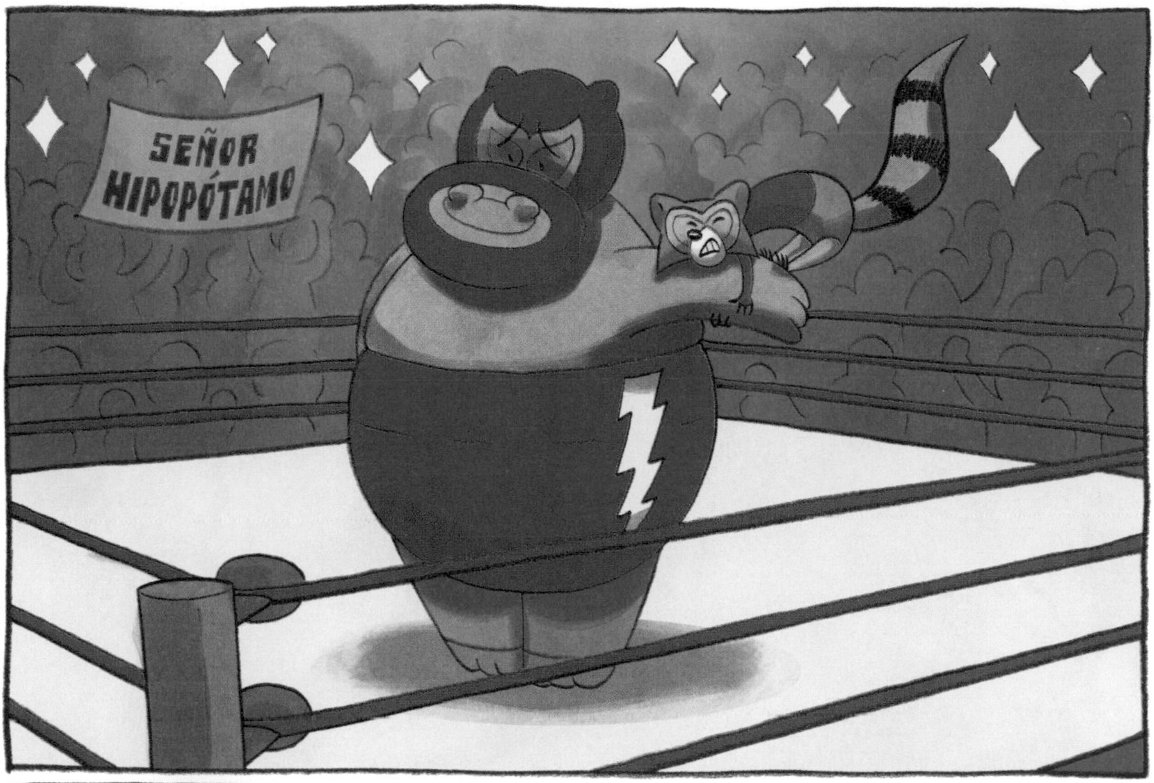
SEÑOR HIPOPÓTAMO

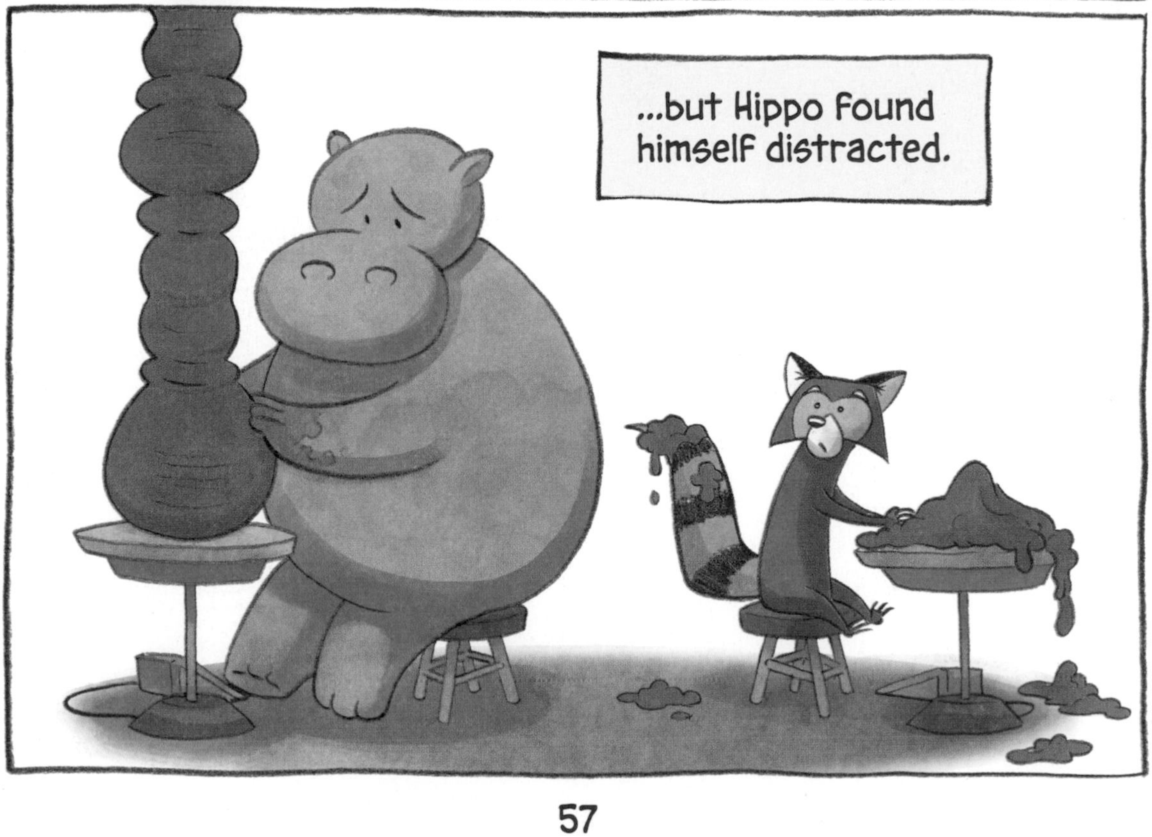
...but Hippo found himself distracted.

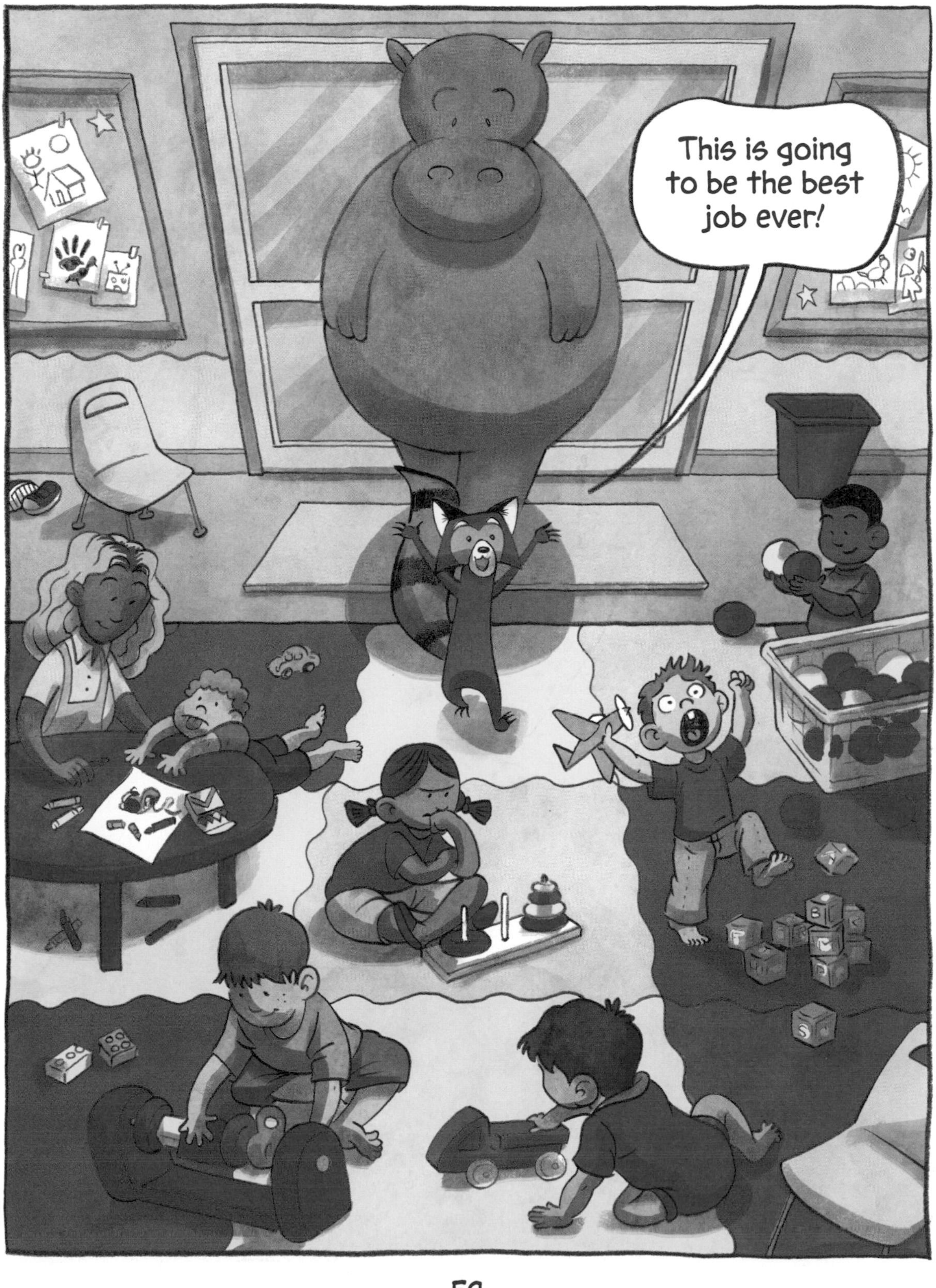
This is going to be the best job ever!

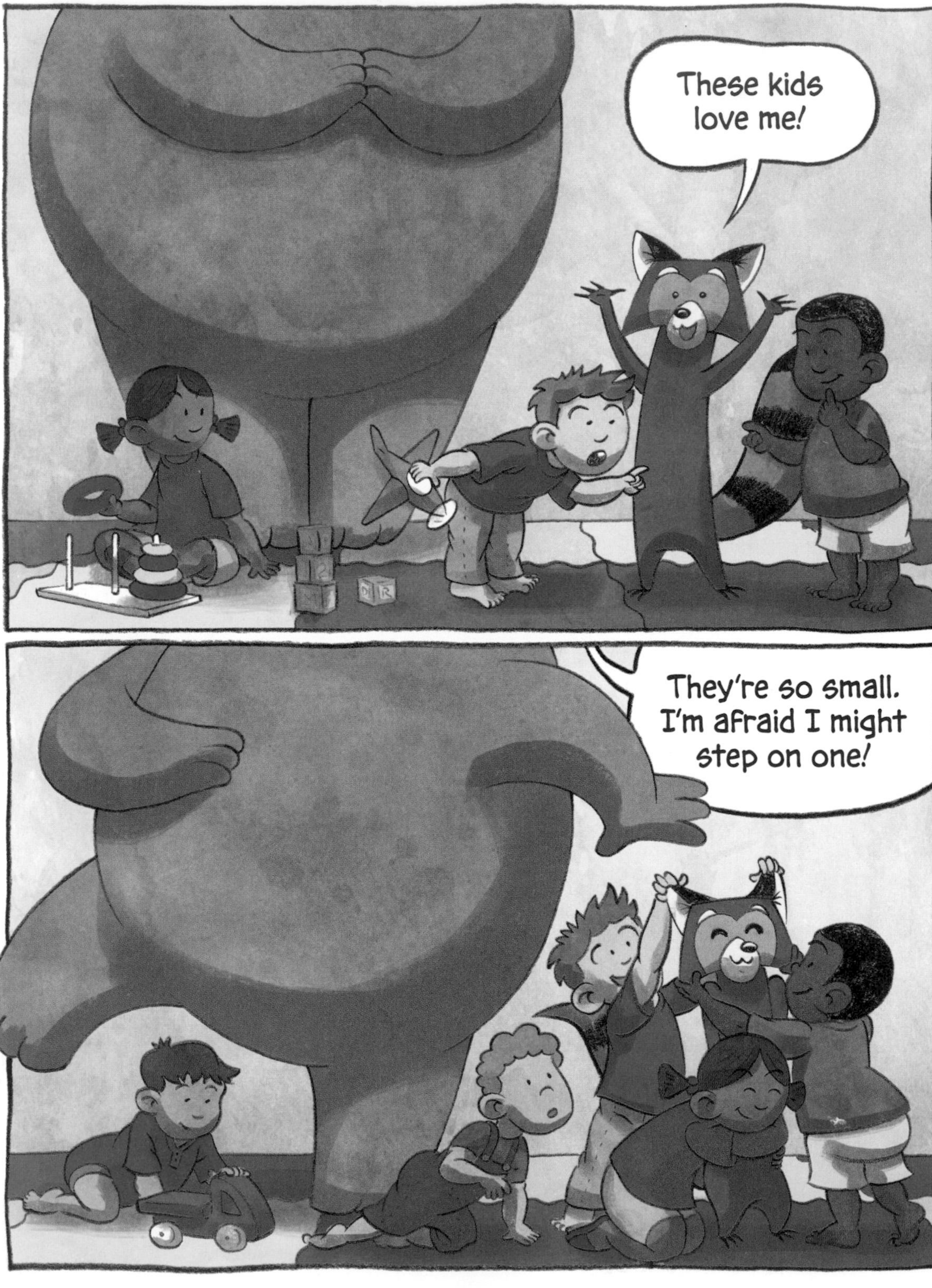
These kids love me!
They're so small. I'm afraid I might step on one!

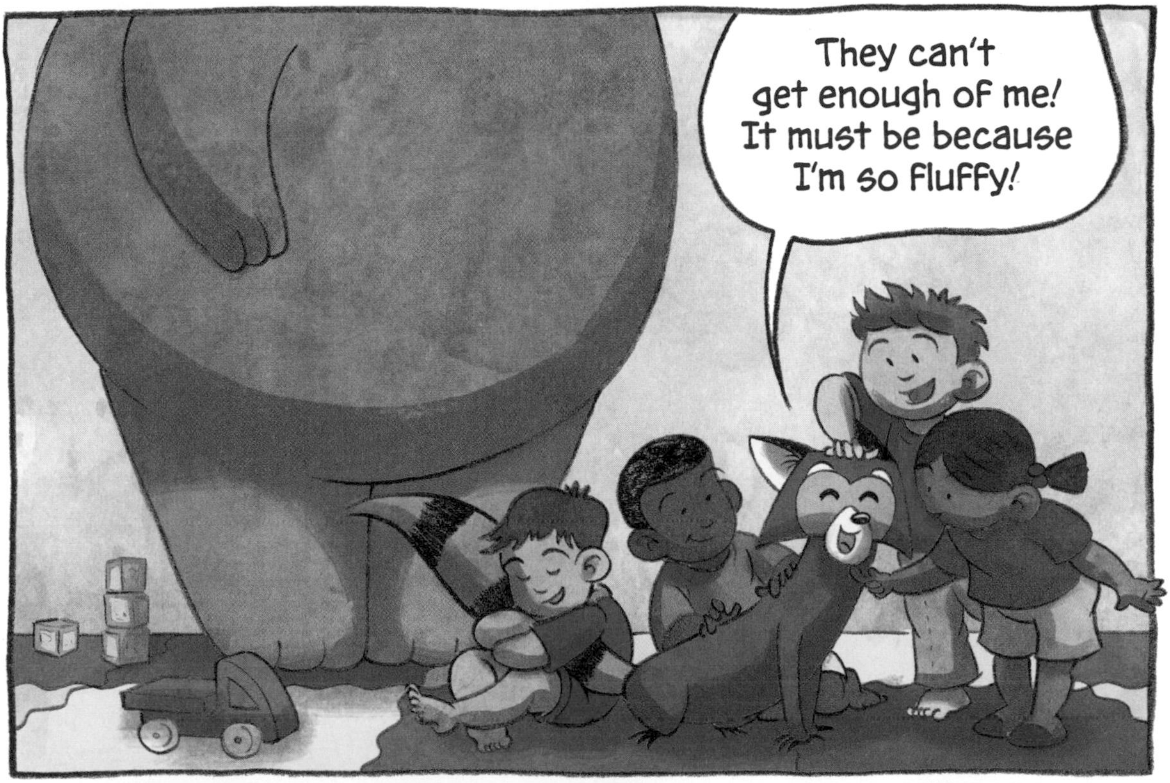
They can't get enough of me! It must be because I'm so fluffy!

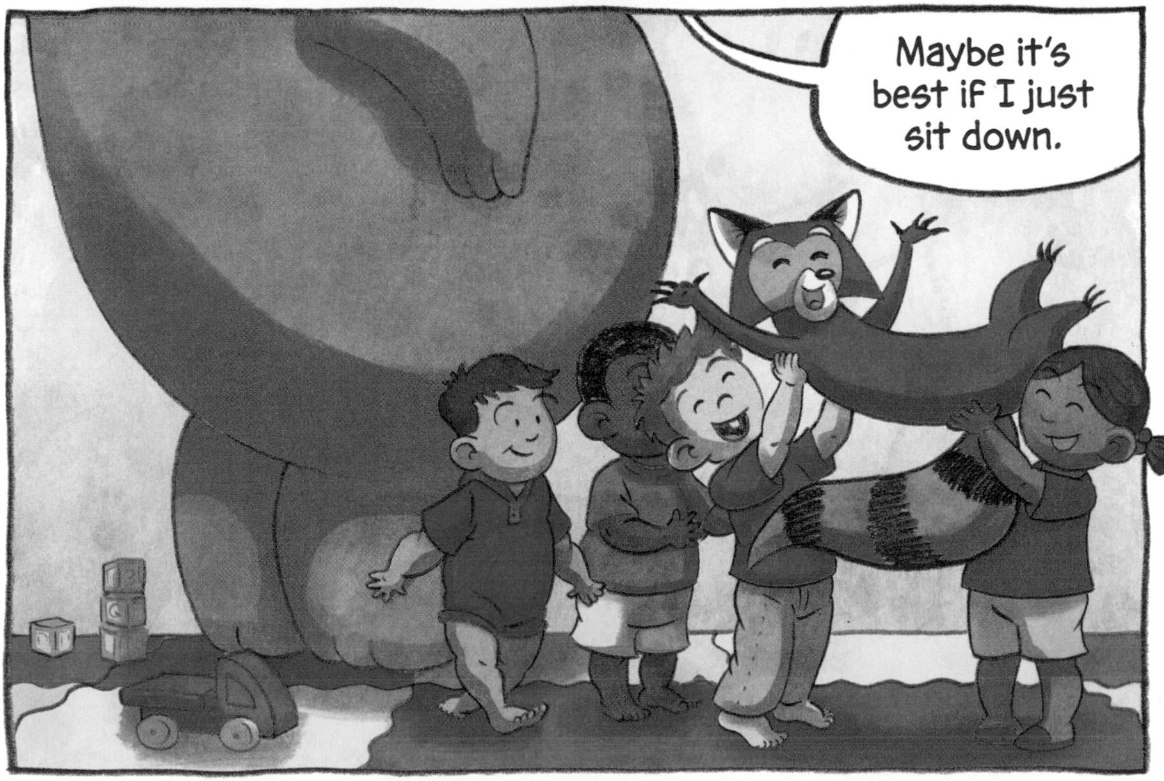
Maybe it's best if I just sit down.

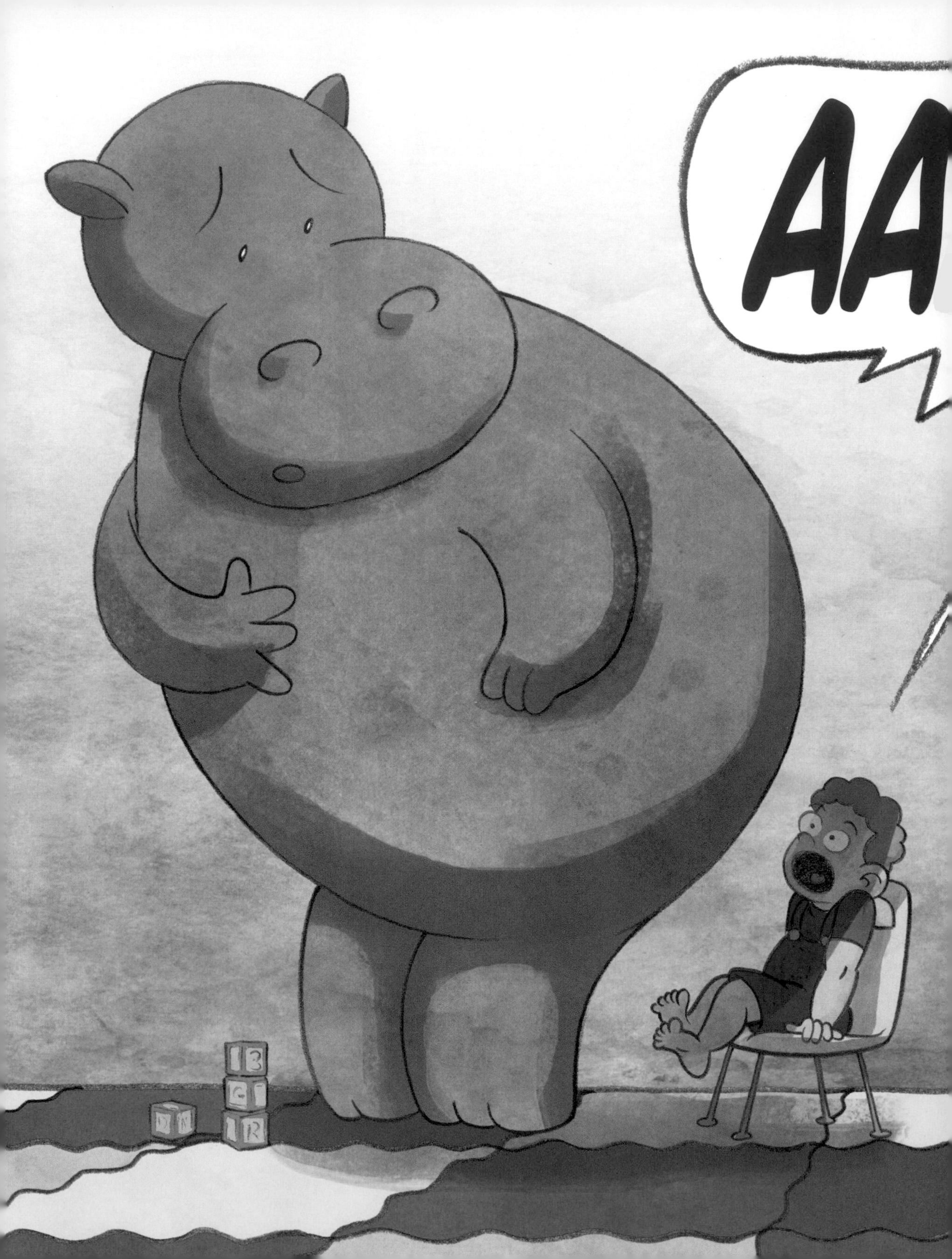
AA

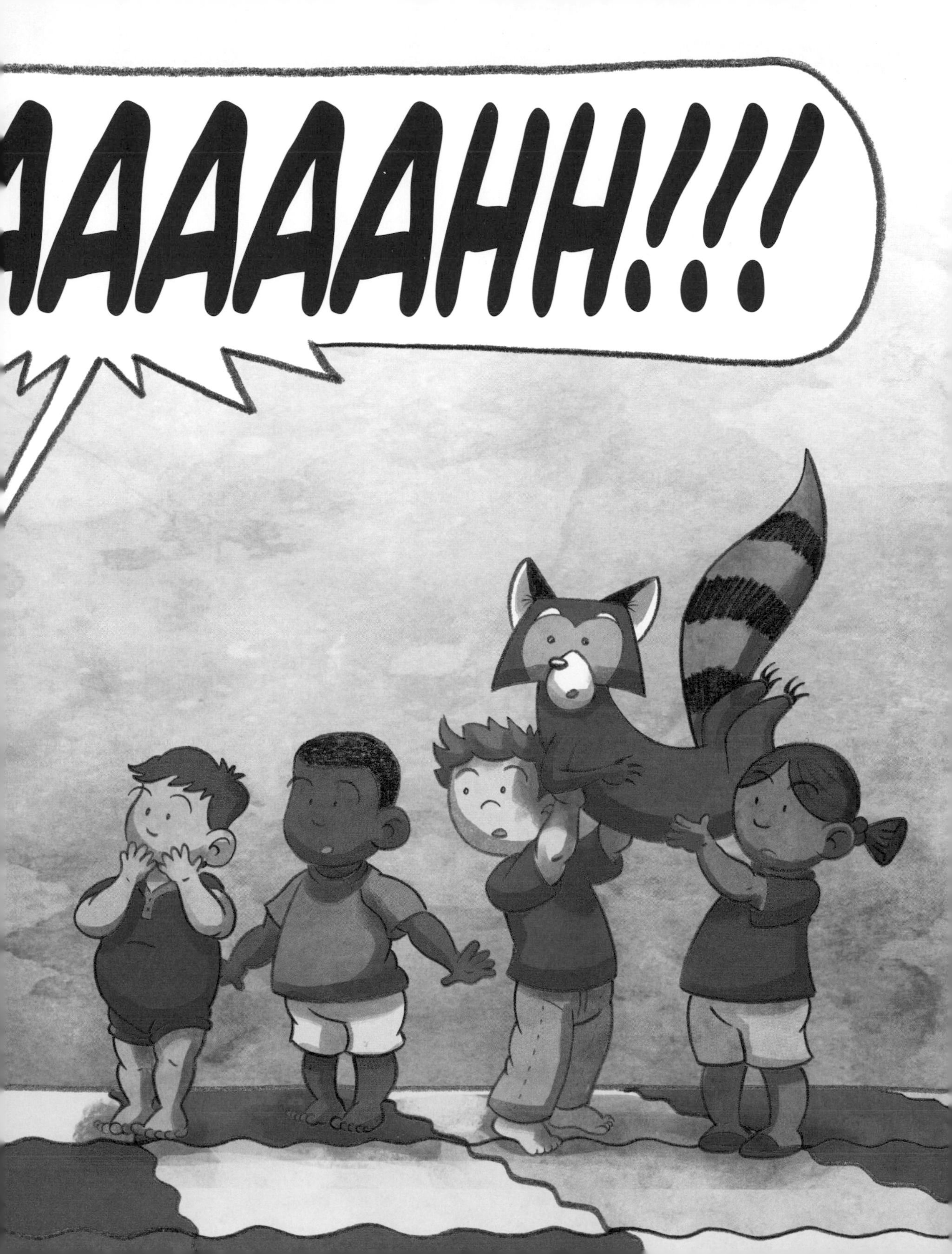
AAAAAAHH!!!

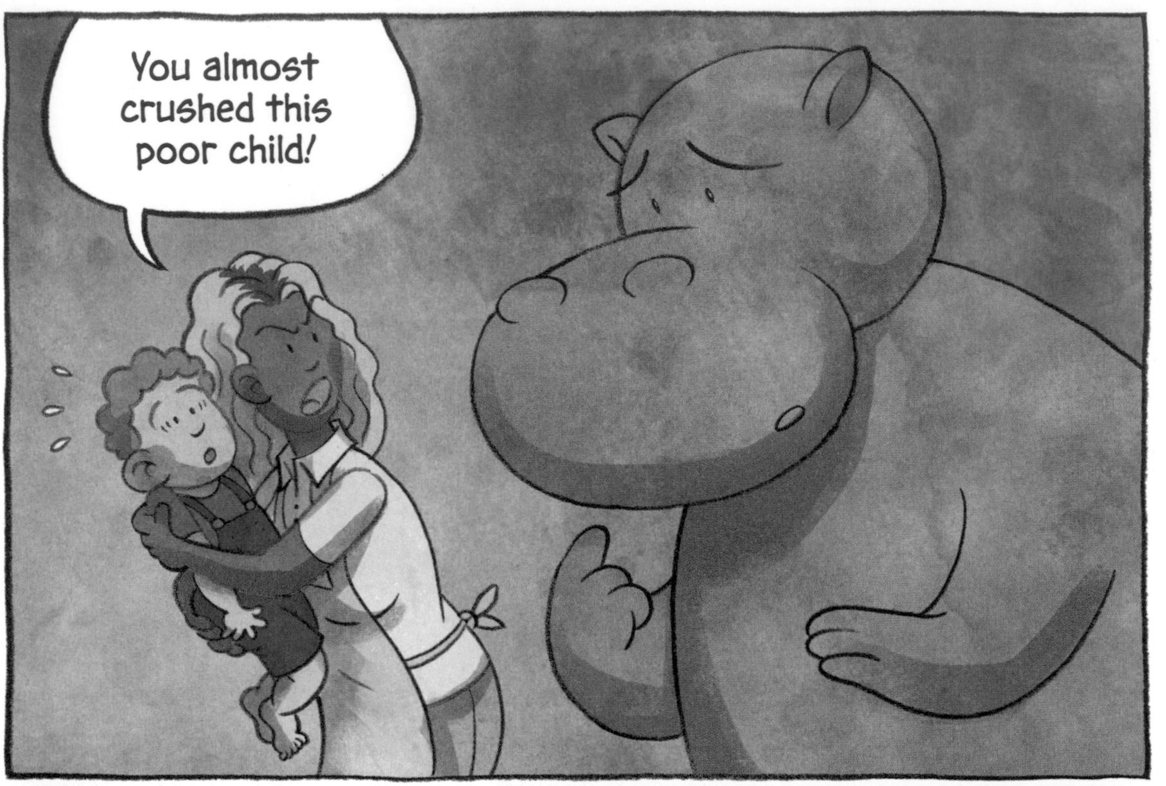
You almost crushed this poor child!

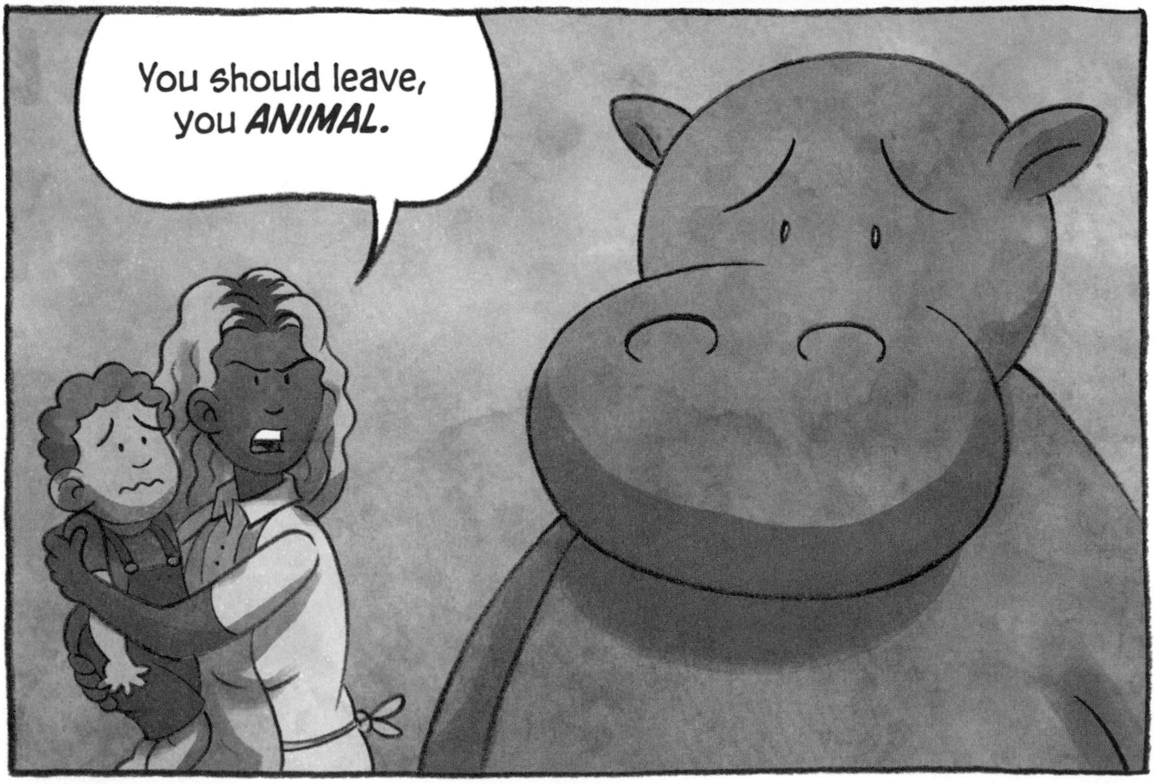
You should leave, you ANIMAL.

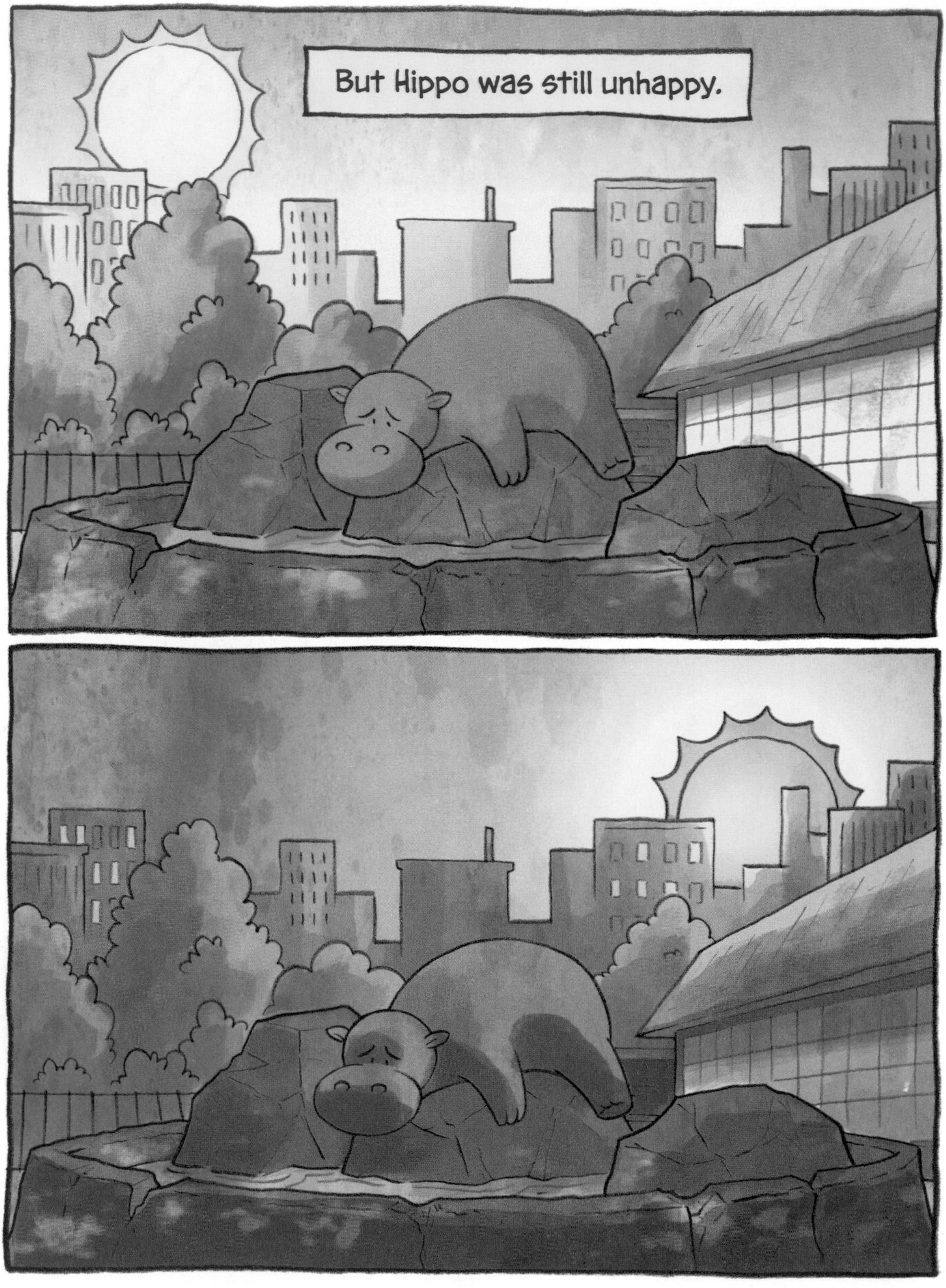
But Hippo was still unhappy.

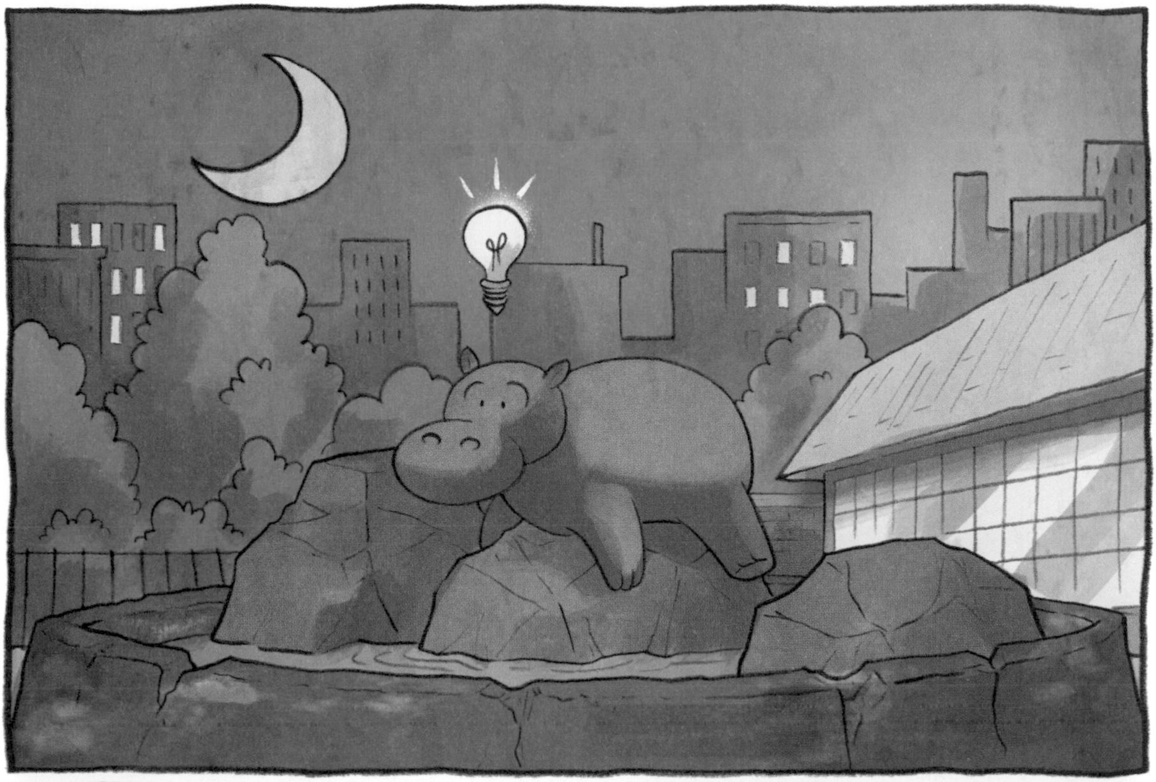

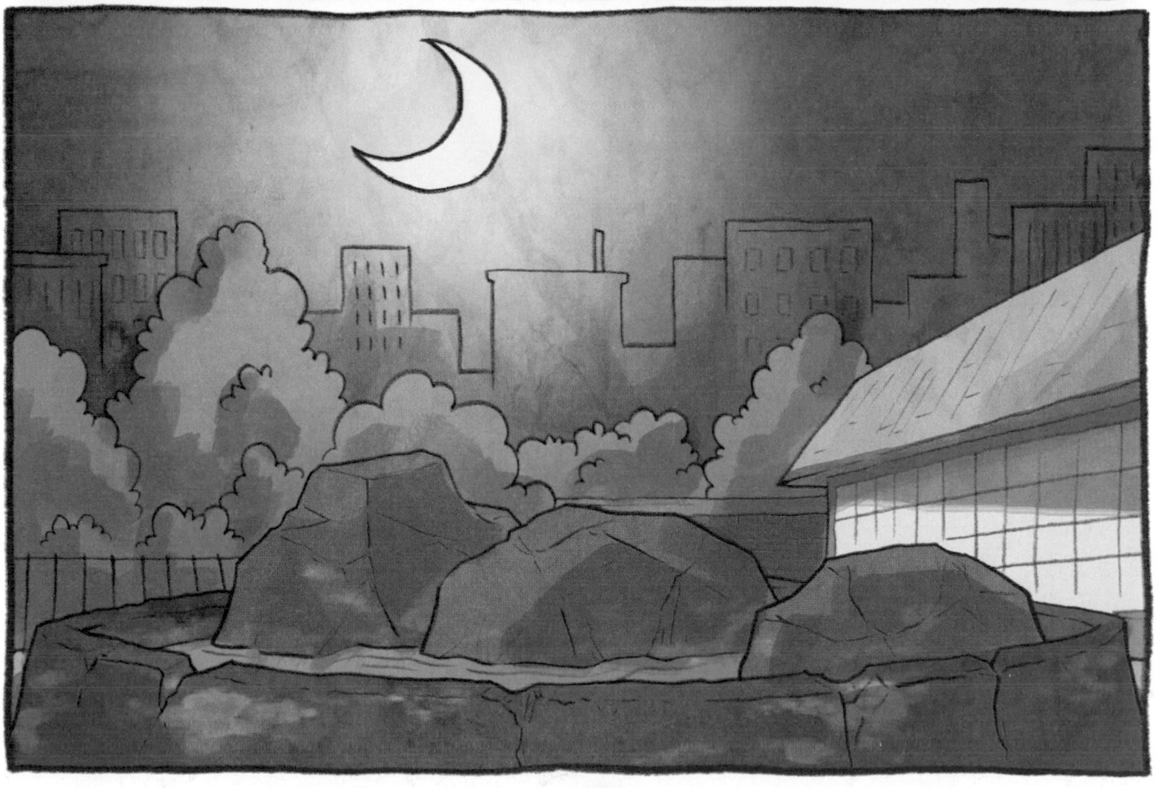

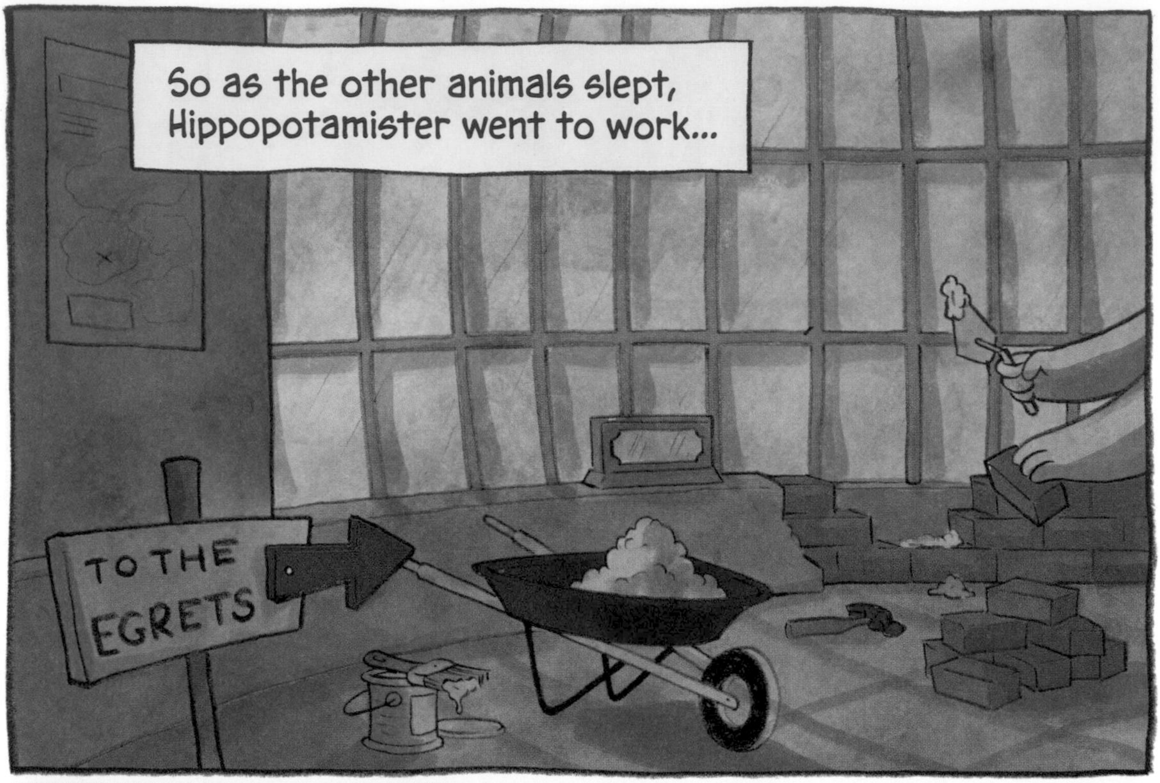
So as the other animals slept, Hippopotamister went to work...
TO THE EGRETS

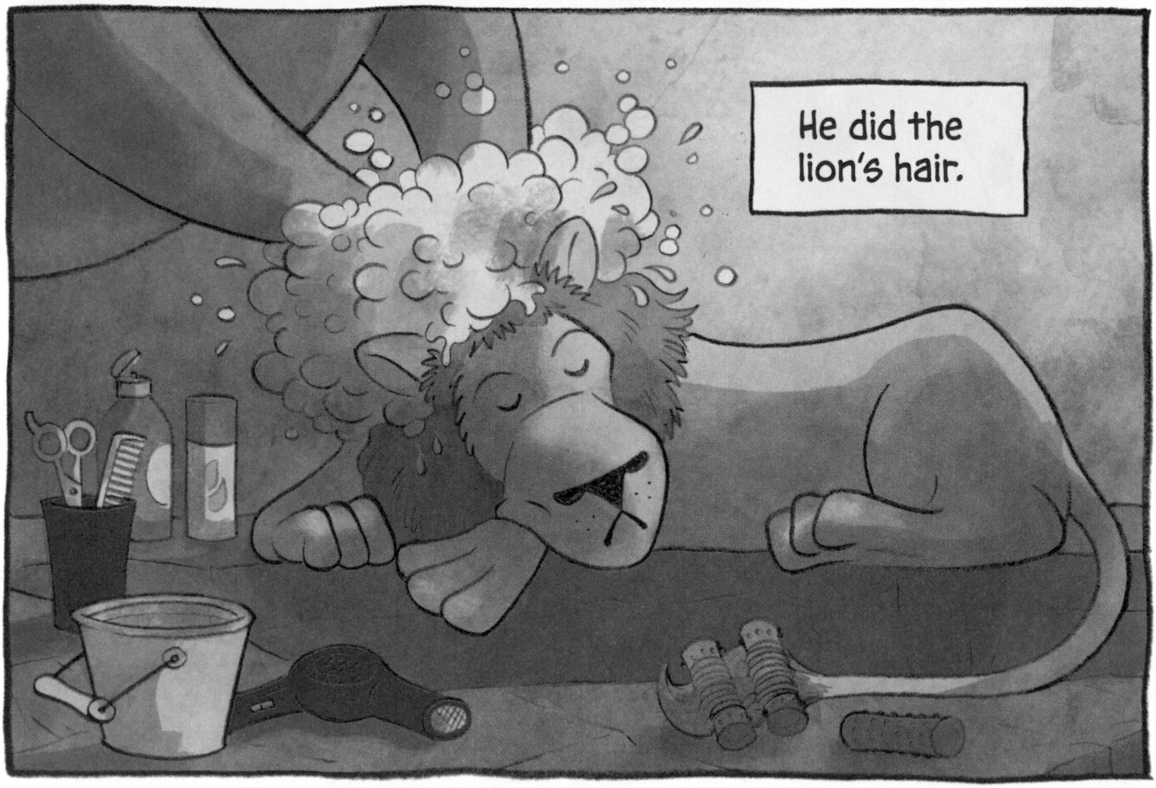
He did the lion's hair.

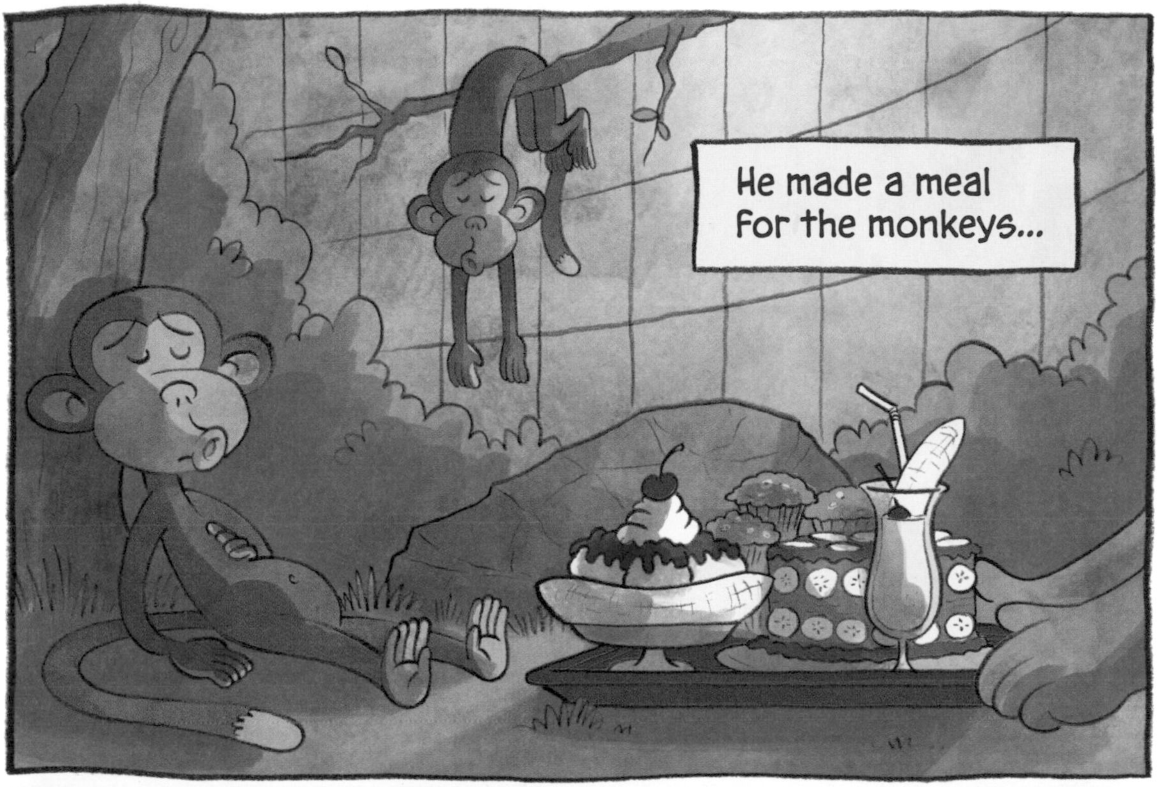
He made a meal
for the monkeys...

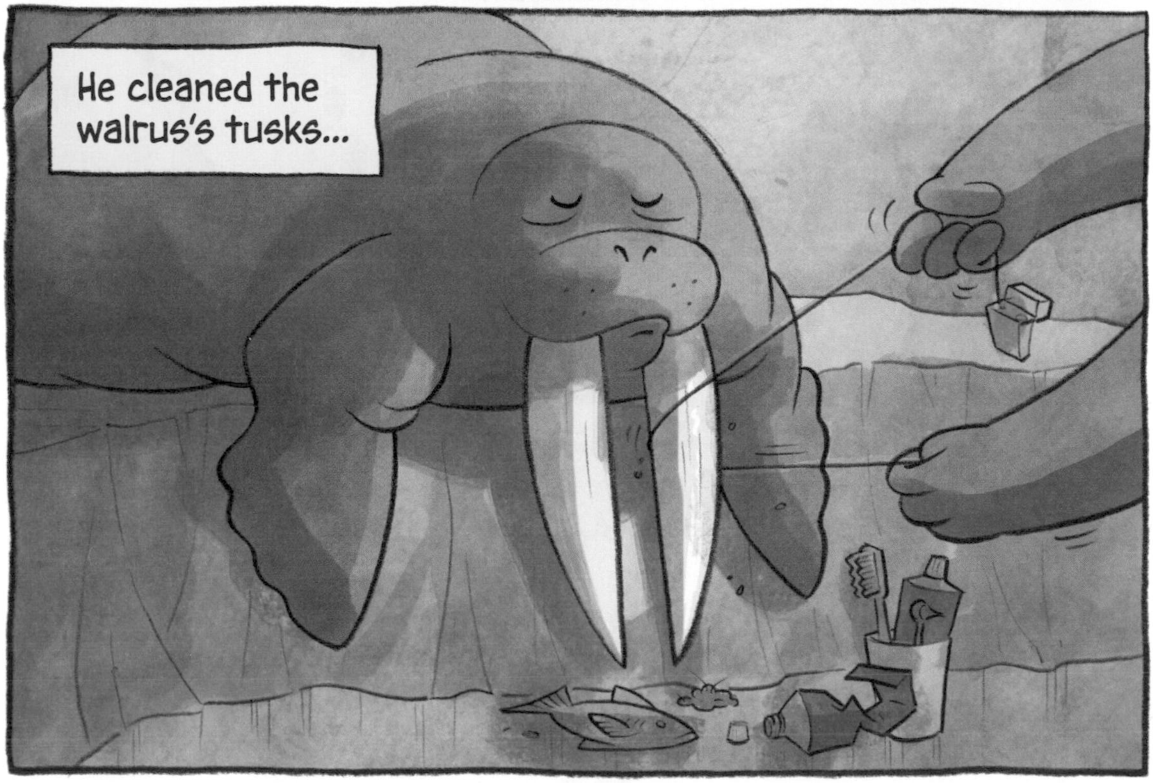
He cleaned the
walrus's tusks...

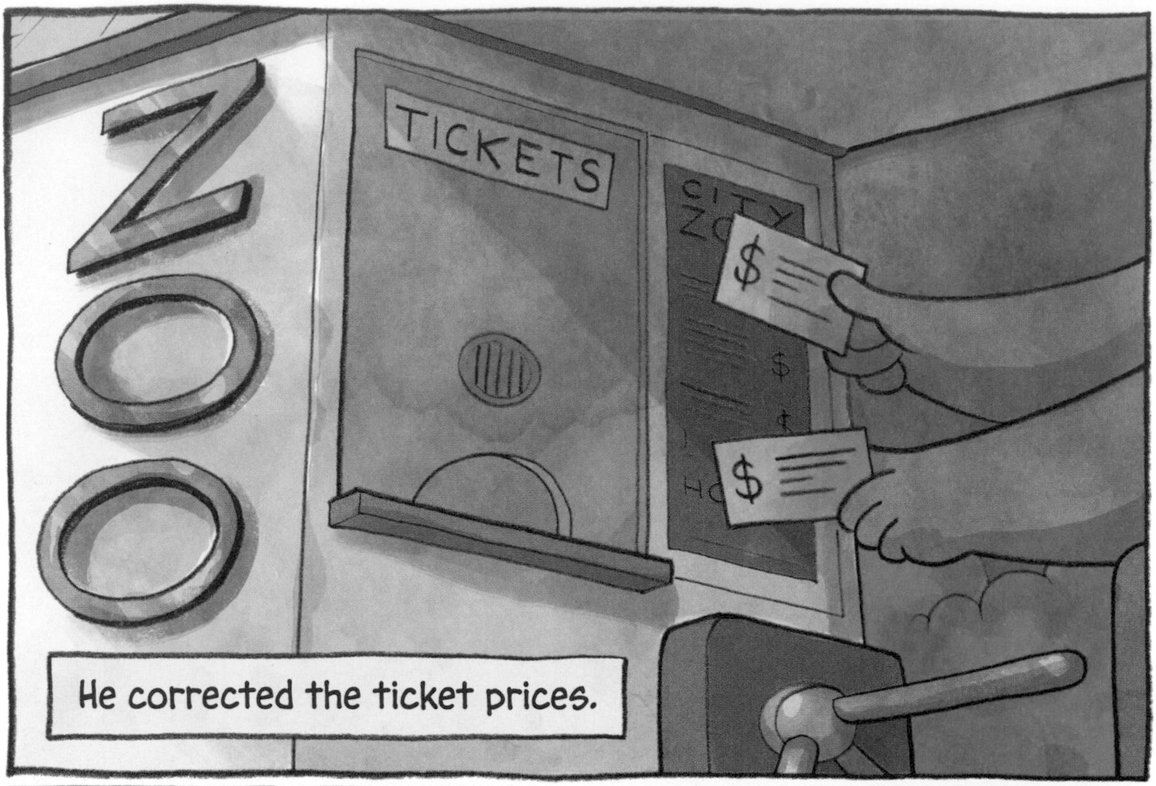
ZOO
TICKETS
He corrected the ticket prices.

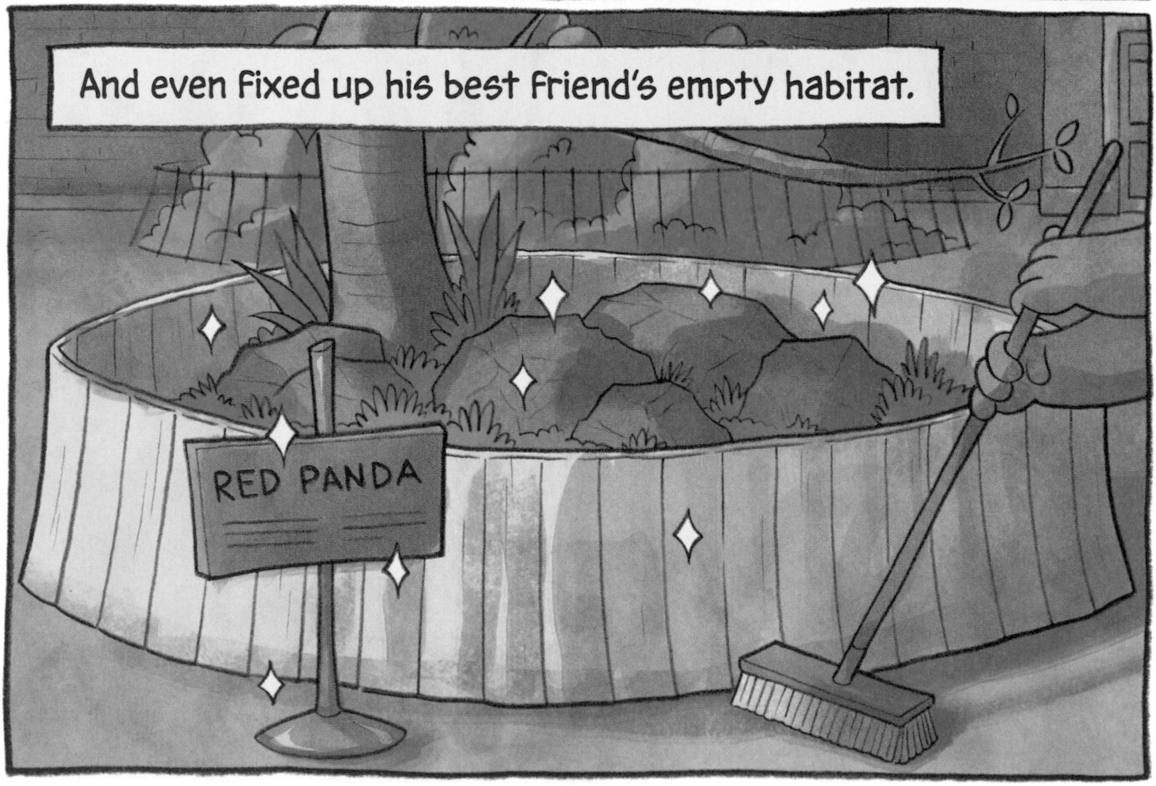
And even fixed up his best friend's empty habitat.
RED PANDA

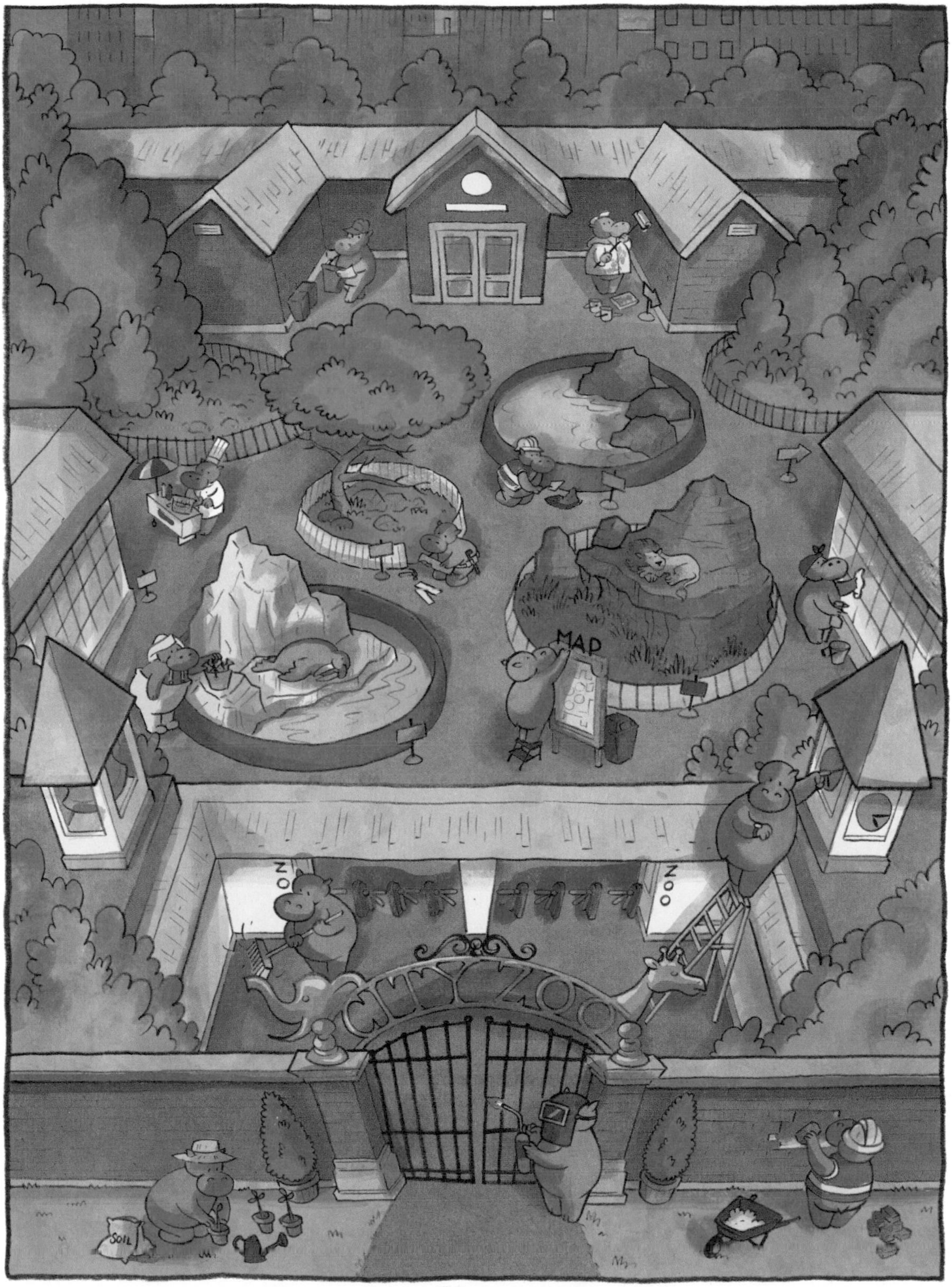
MAP
ZOO
ZOO
CITY ZOO
SOIL

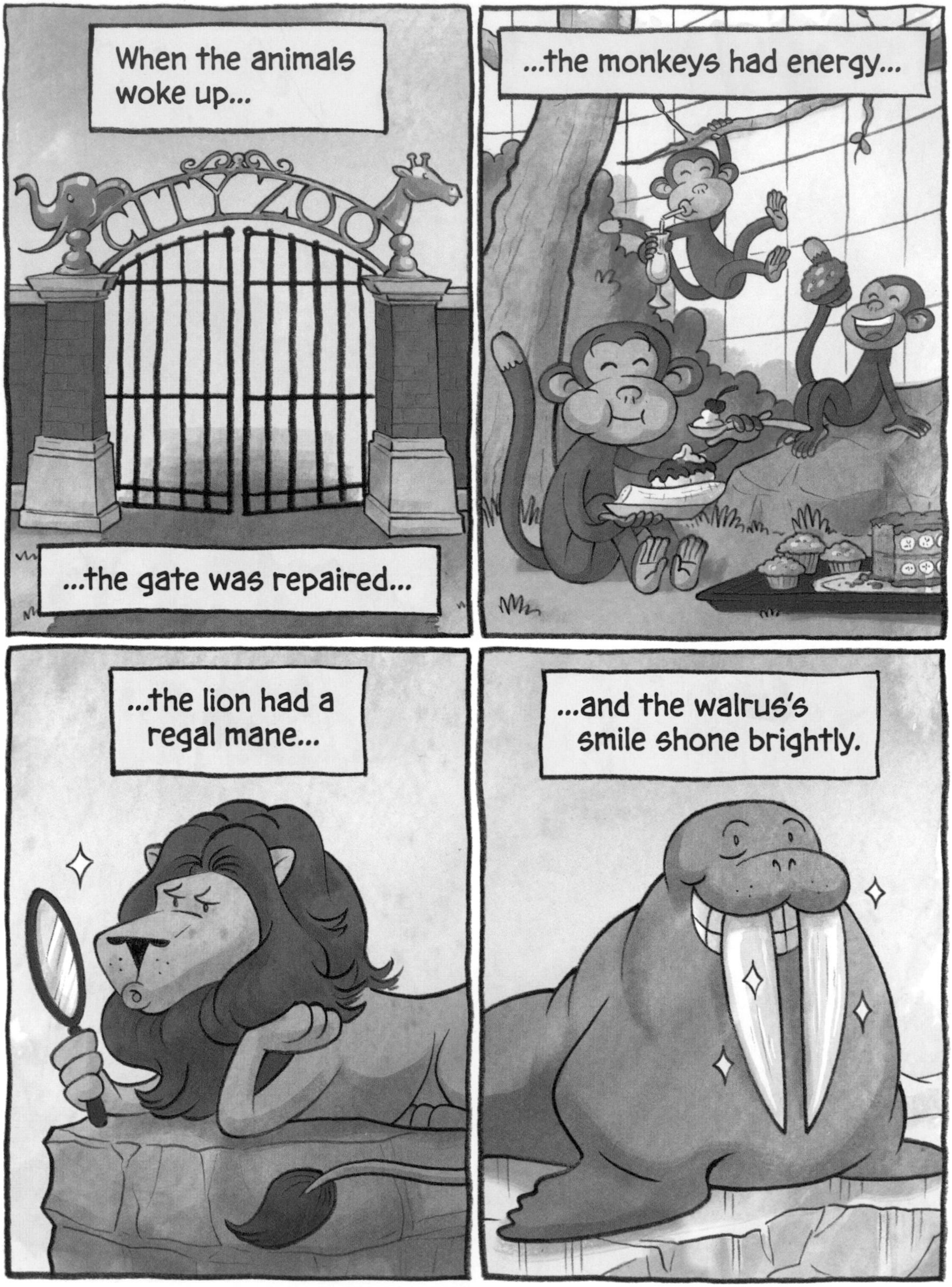
When the animals woke up...
CITY ZOO
...the gate was repaired...
...the monkeys had energy...
...the lion had a regal mane...
...and the walrus's smile shone brightly.

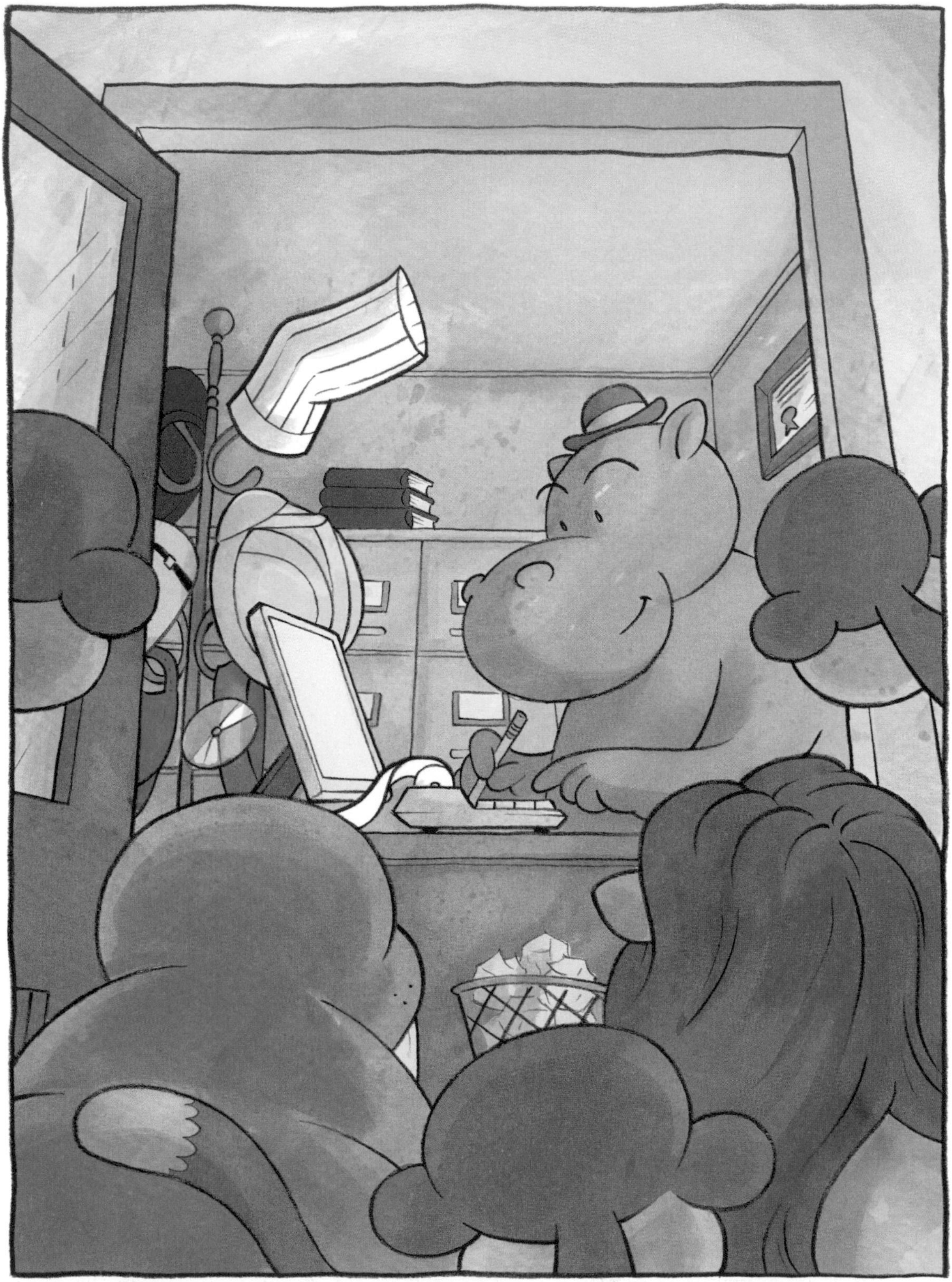

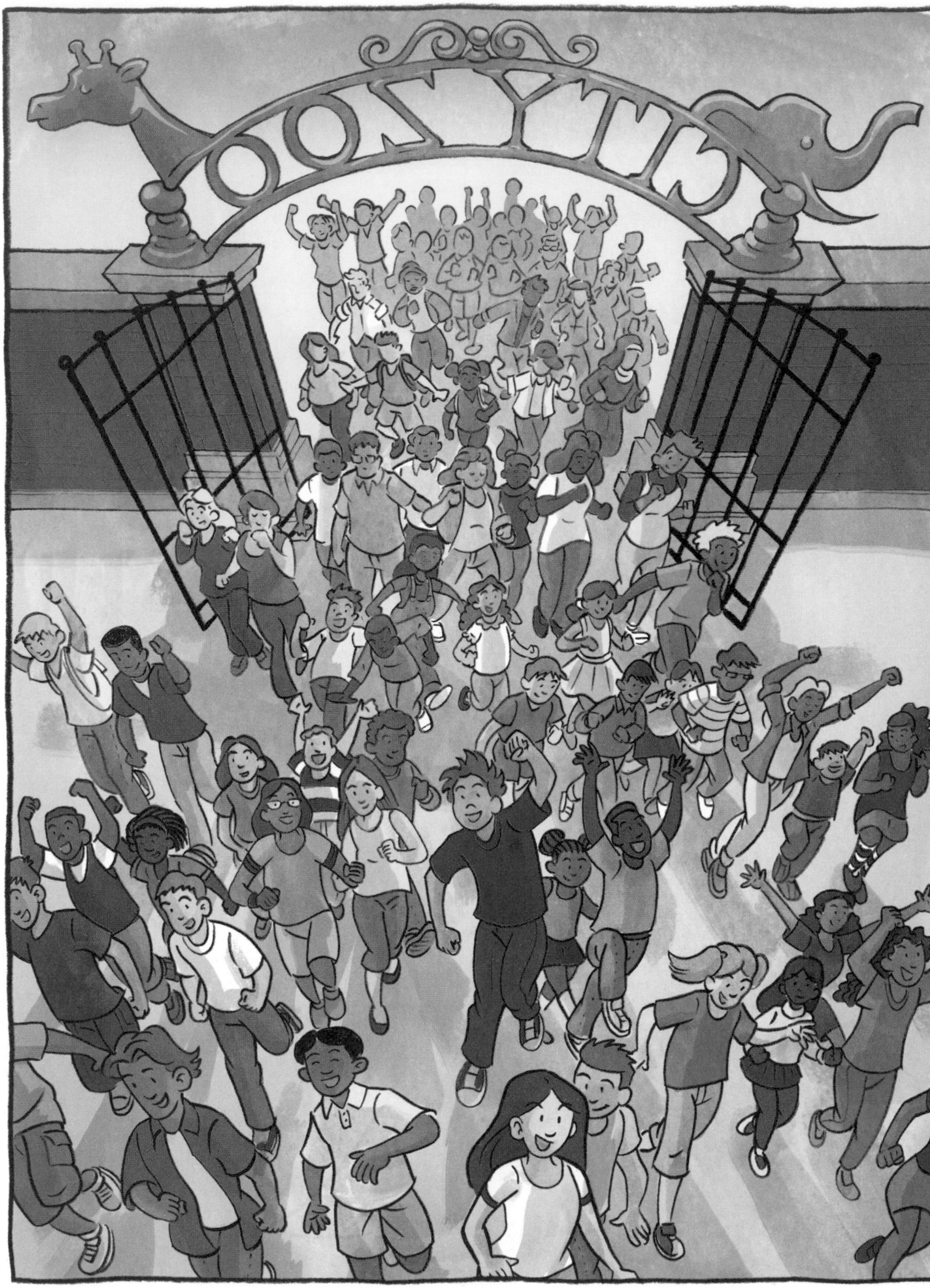

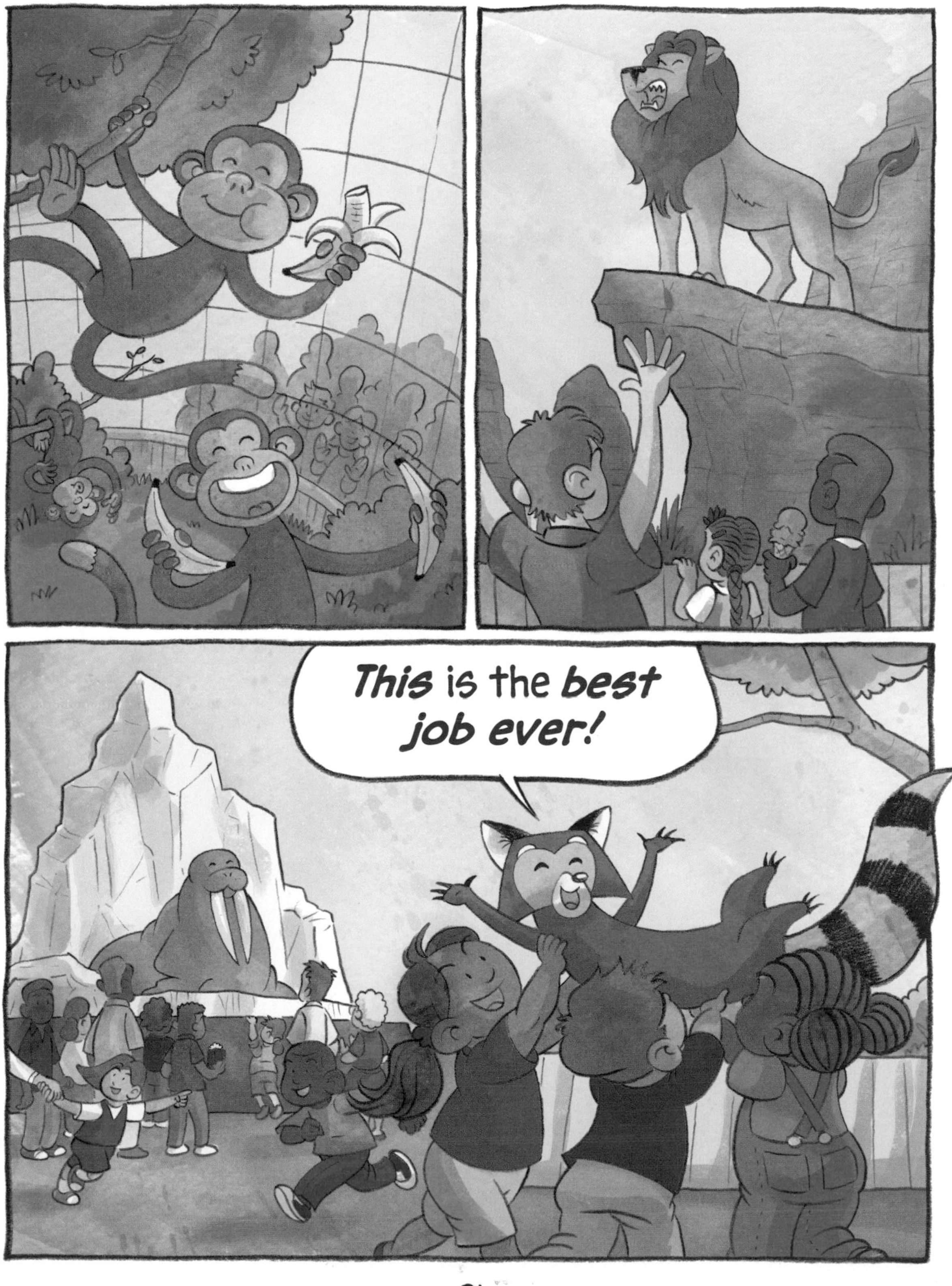
This is the best job ever!

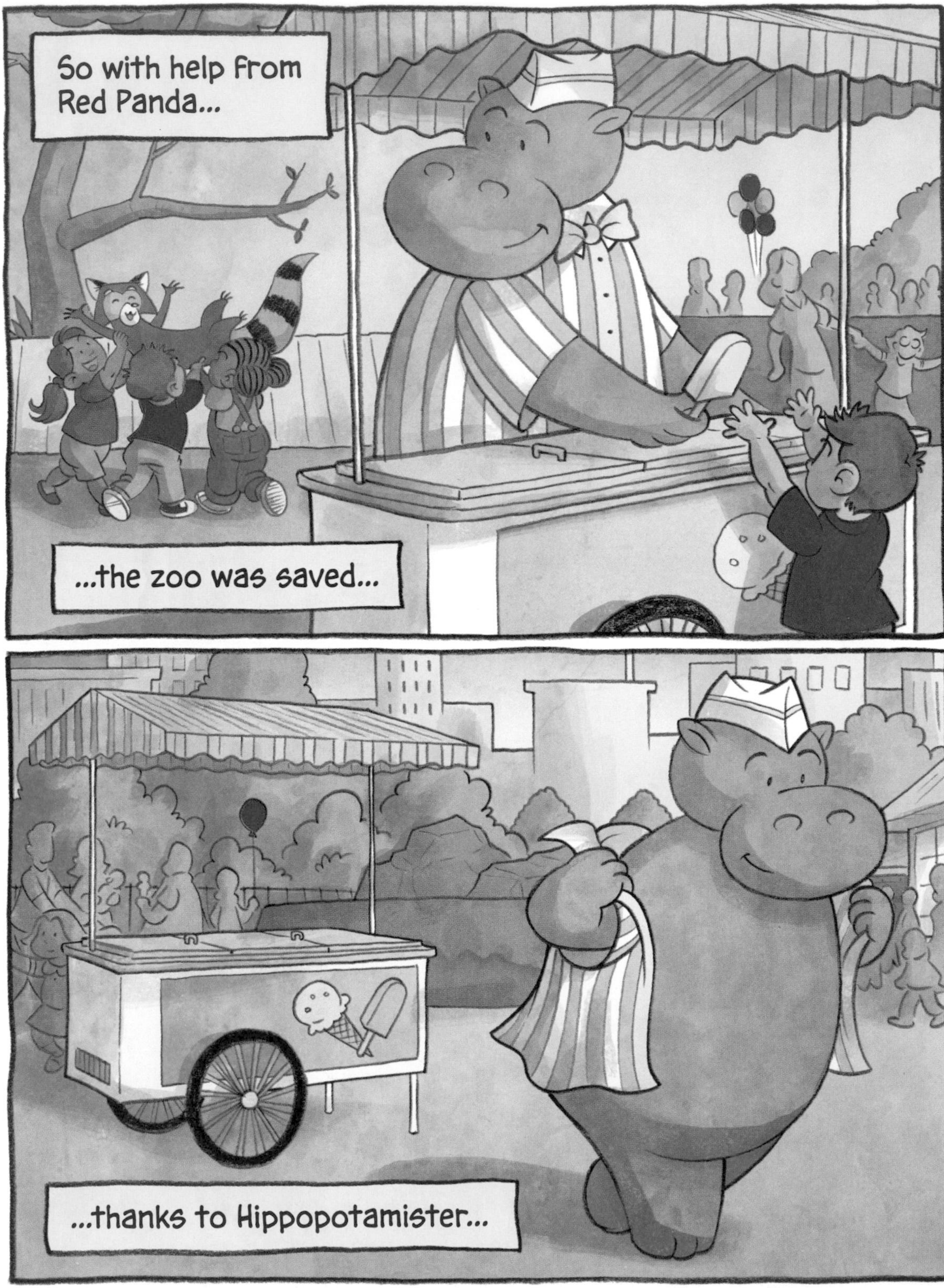
So with help from Red Panda...
...the zoo was saved...
...thanks to Hippopotamister...

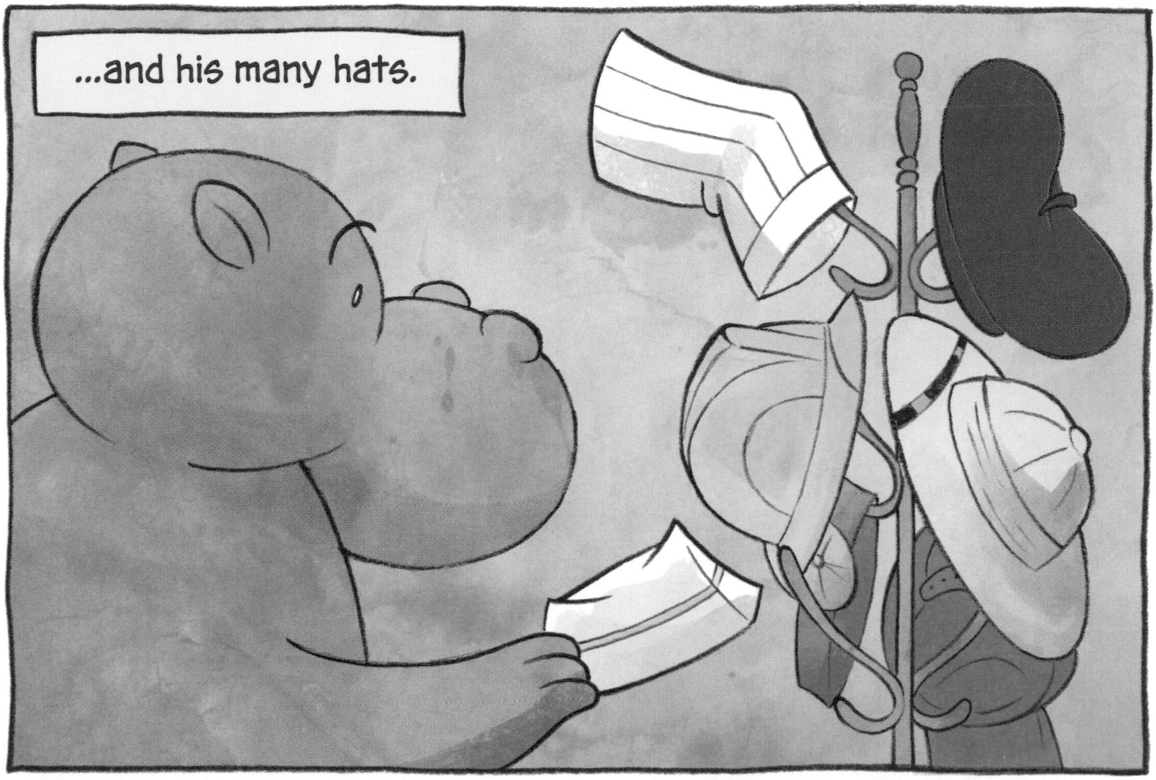
...and his many hats.

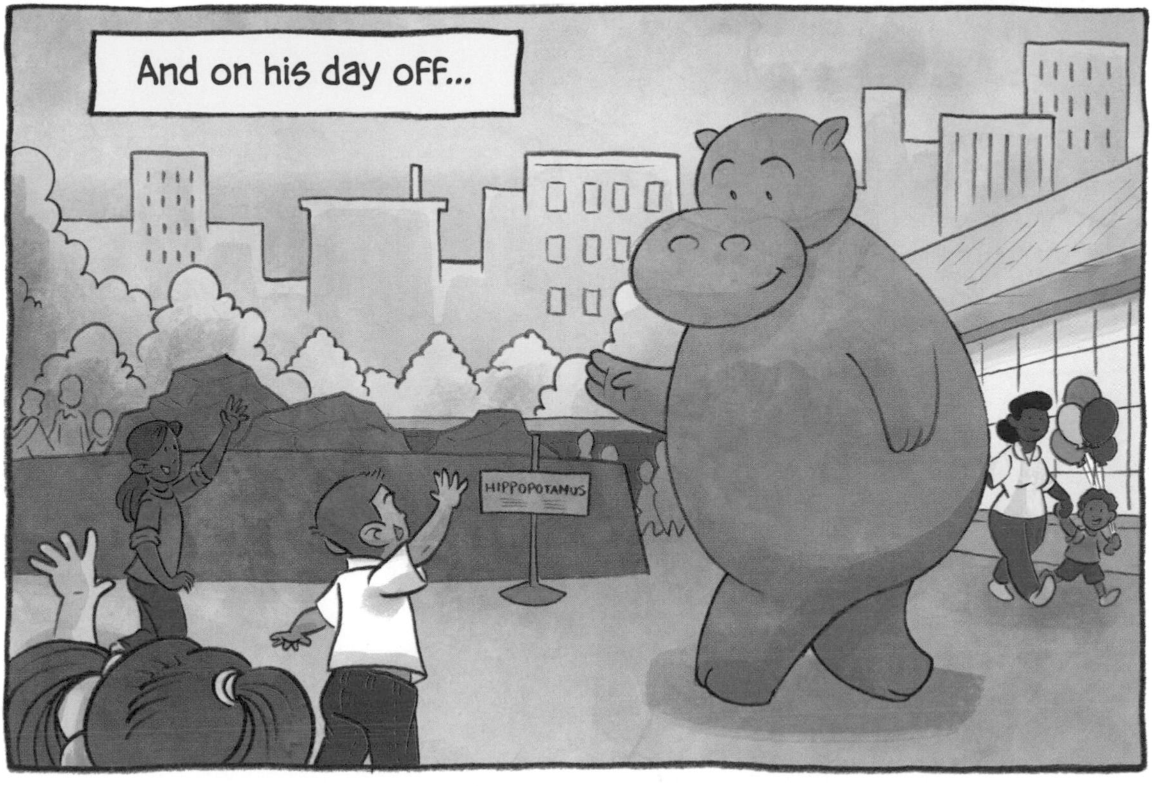
And on his day off...
HIPPOPOTAMUS

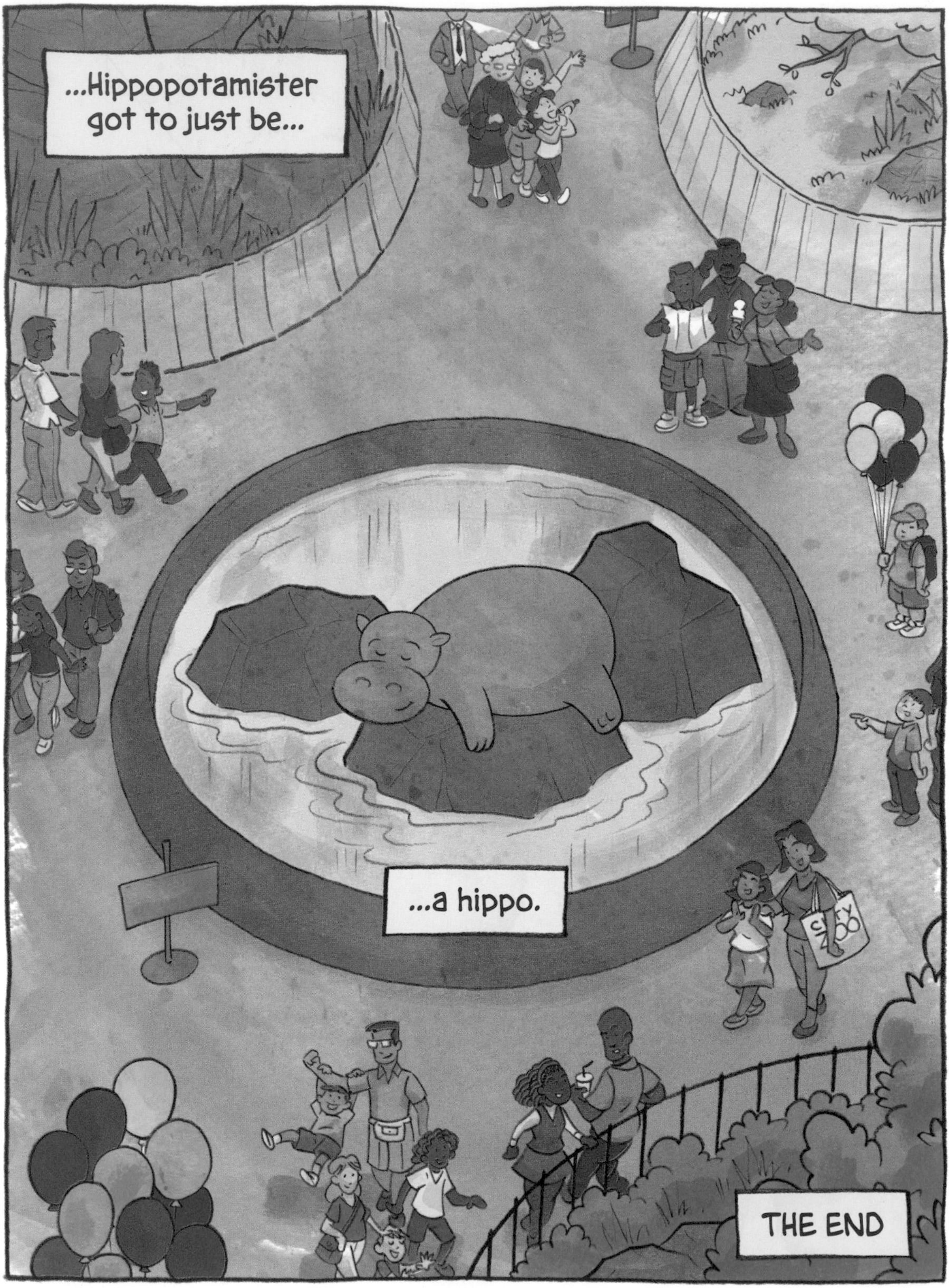
...Hippopotamister got to just be...
...a hippo.
THE END

How to draw HIPPOPOTAMISTER

1) Start with a circle, high up where his head should be.

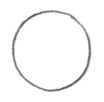

2) Draw an oval slightly overlapping the circle for his snout.

3) Draw a large egg shape for his body.

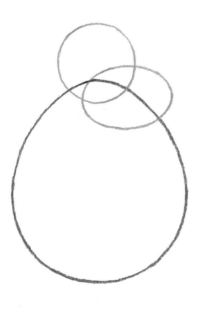

4) Add a trapezoid (a rectangle with angled sides) at the bottom for his legs.

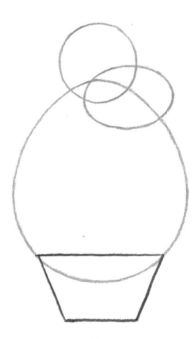

5) Draw details like his ears, eyes, nostrils, arms, and toes.

6) Erase any unwanted lines.

Finally, give Hippopotamister a hat. He's got a lot to choose from!

How to draw RED PANDA

1) Start with a trapezoid for his head. Draw lightly because Red Panda needs more erasing than Hippopotamister.

2) Draw a long tube shape for his body, almost like a hot dog.

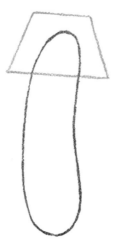

3) Add a small egg shape for his snout and triangles for his ears.

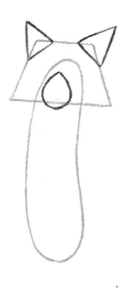

4) His arms, legs, and tail are more complex shapes and might take practice.

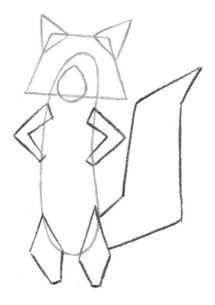

5) Draw details like his ears, eyes, mouth, fingers, toes, and tail stripes.

6) Fill in his ears and tail stripes and erase any unwanted lines.

Red Panda likes hats, too. Don't forget to add his best friend Hippo!

Special thanks—
to my family; to Calista Brill, Gina Gagliano, Danielle Ceccolini, Mark Siegel,
and Colleen AF Venable; to Cat for her amazing colors; to Dave Roman,
Raina Telgemeier, Jerzy Drozd, Zack Giallongo, and all my friends in comics;
to *Geek Mom*, *Mr. Schu Reads*, *The Beat*, *SLJ Good Comics for Kids*, *Geek Dad*,
Seven Impossible Things Before Breakfast, and *Nerdy Book Club*;
to librarians, teachers, and booksellers;
and to adorable animals everywhere.

First Second

Hippopotamister was drawn on Strathmore Bristol vellum with Staedtler 2B, 3B, and 6B pencils,
and digitally colored in Photoshop.

Published by First Second
First Second is an imprint of Roaring Brook Press,
a division of Holtzbrinck Publishing Holdings Limited Partnership
175 Fifth Avenue, New York, New York 10010
All rights reserved

Library of Congress Control Number: 2015944386

ISBN 978-1-62672-200-2

Our books may be purchased in bulk for promotional, educational, or business use. Please
contact your local bookseller or the Macmillan Corporate and Premium Sales Department at
(800) 221-7945 ext. 5442 or by e-mail at MacmillanSpecialSales@macmillan.com.

FIRST

EDITION

First edition 2016
Book design by John Green
Printed in China by Toppan Leefung Printing Ltd., Dongguan City, Guangdong Province

1 3 5 7 9 10 8 6 4 2

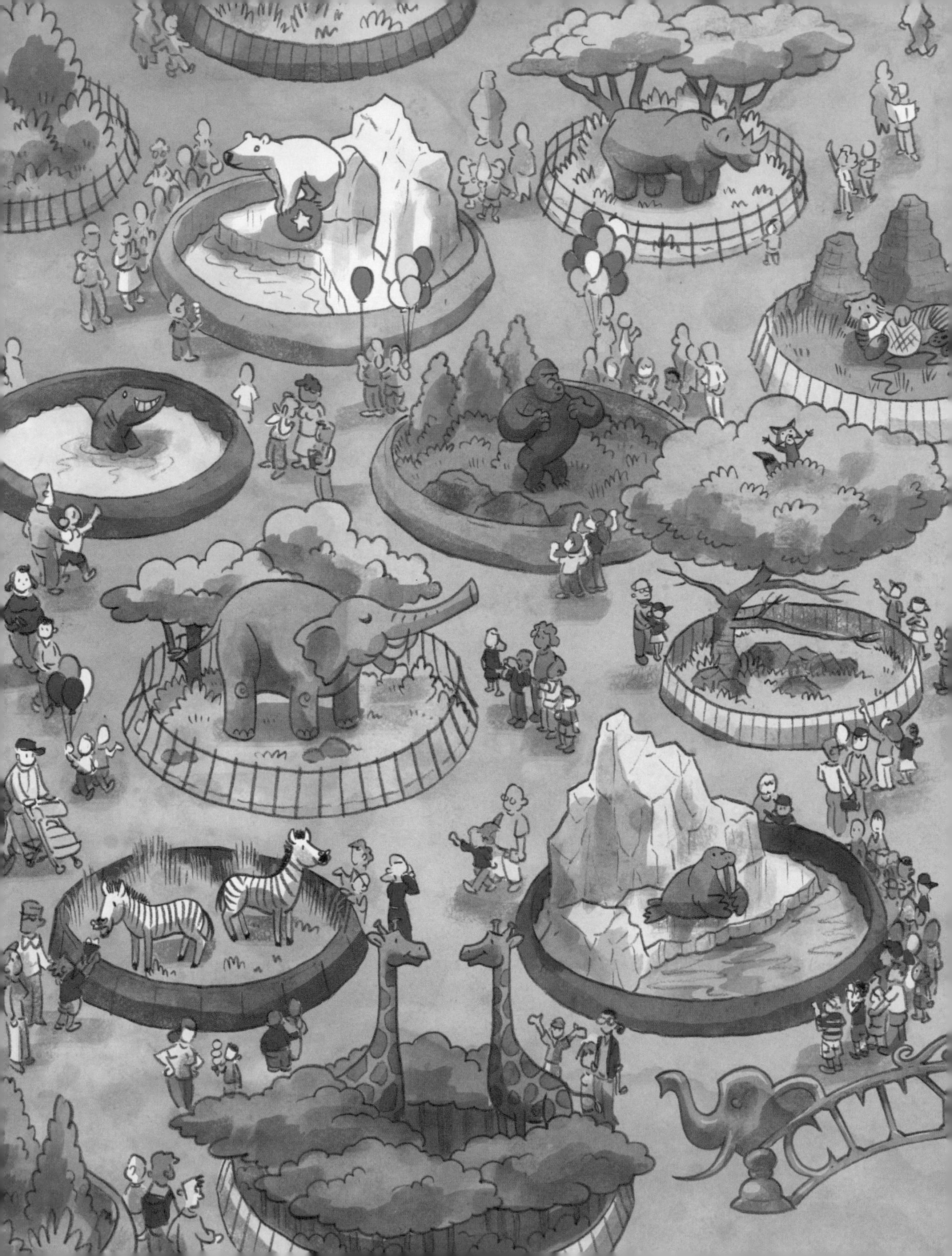